REAPING BOOK ONE

Ephesus

CHRISTIS CHRISTIE

Midnight Tide
PUBLISHING

Spun Gold: A Rumpelstiltskin Origin Story

Blood From a Stone: A Villain's Anthology

Cirque de vol Mystique: A Circus Anthology

Something in the Shadows: A Halloween Anthology

Immortal Realms Trilogy:
    Seeds of Sorrow (Coming 2022)
    Tides of Torment (Coming Soon)
    Wages of War (Coming Soon)

PROLOGUE

A BRIGHT PETAL ON THE WIND

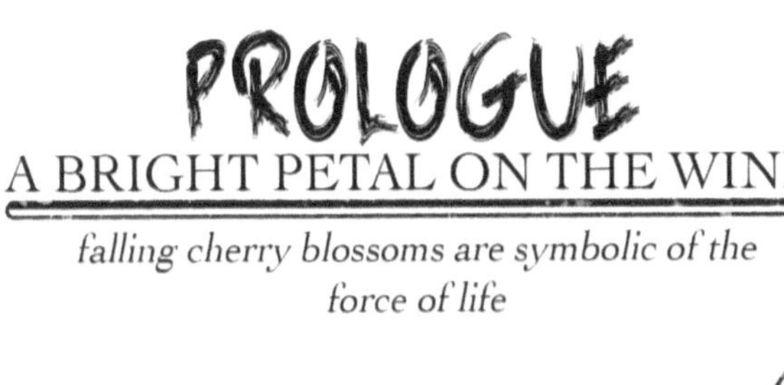

falling cherry blossoms are symbolic of the force of life

The Creator loved to watch the brightly burning lights as they drifted down towards earth. A gentle breeze of falling petals until their final destination was chosen, then a more determined fall. Swift flashes of blue to signify the body had been accepting of the soul, then life began. Some souls shimmered more brightly than the others, and those souls the Creator would keep an eye on. Watching their growth and then eventual birth, smiling as their shrill wails filled the air with new spirit, and tiny fists created miniature cyclones of energy.

Watching their first steps, hearing their first words, and seeing them develop into the important people that the Creator had intended for them to be. Fulfilling a great destiny determined before they had even taken the journey from the Forever, down into life. Once it was time for their journey on earth to end, the Creator lovingly welcomed those who had lived beautifully back into the Forever. Others were left to slumber in a tormented sleep until they were ready to be called back.

Some, though, the Creator had to watch aimlessly wander the earth, searching for a life unfulfilled or clinging to earthly treasures that were now lost to them, beyond their reach. It saddened the Creator greatly, but until they were settled, they were out of reach. That was until the day a petal fell that shone more brightly than any others, one that the Creator had an especially important destiny determined for.

The Creator watched, pleased, as the soul chose the perfect mother and nestled warmly within her womb. As the soul grew, the Creator observed with fondness the care and love granted to the small, blossoming life, who was awaited so expectantly by the family it had chosen. Many great things would come from this new, burgeoning life. New advances, lives saved, people freed. This soul would be a gift from the Creator to the lives of those in its homeland, a new beacon of light for the living.

However, some things even the Creator could not control. One night, as the bright soul's parents journeyed home from a town farther away, they were beset by nefarious men. The Creator could only watch, as the actions of humans were a free and unseen thing. In tragedy, the bright soul's mother lost her life, and with her, so too did the little life fade away.

The Creator mourned with a deep sadness for what had been stolen away, as the mother's light drifted up towards the Forever. The bright little soul made to follow, but something kept it hovering over the earth, afraid to follow and leave behind what hadn't been lived. Not wishing to see the bright soul become another of the lost, the Creator drew close, surrounding it. The bright soul was given a new purpose, and through that purpose, to live but not to live. To see but not to be seen. To collect the lost souls for the Creator and return them to the deep sleep until they could finally be called home.

The bright soul accepted this new appointment, and he became known as Ephesus.

CHAPTER ONE
A PAPAVER PLUCKED

*poppies are a symbol of remembrance,
sacrifice & death*

Korea

"So, you have returned, Jug-eum. Is it finally time for you to collect me?" Sun-hee's voice rasped wearily from the bed on the floor, the covers doing little to conceal the frailty of her form.

"Good evening, Sun-hee." I stooped to sit beside her pallet, legs crossed beneath me, and adjusted the lengthy, black robes that I wore. Souls typically remained wearing the garment they had died in. I, however, had never worn anything upon my body. Instead, my form was shrouded in floor-length robes that concealed my thin frame.

I hadn't thought Sun-hee would be conscious enough to see me this time, but she was stubborn and held on to life. "Tonight is the night. But I have no need to collect you. You are ready to pass on to the Forever," I murmured softly, hands folded respectfully in my lap.

It wasn't my custom to converse with those who were on the verge of death, unless they needed convincing to fade into the darkness that awaited them. Sun-hee was not one such needy soul, perfectly content to accept death when it finally came. But she had been awake each time I came to this home, and in those moments, she had spoken frankly and without concern to me.

It pleased me to find her awake now in these last minutes.

Sun-hee's soul glowed warm and golden, coursing through her with a vitality that directly opposed the weakness of her mortal flesh. She would not last through the night, but this did not alter her peace.

"Then you do an old lady a courtesy call to say farewell?"

I smiled softly, shaking my head. Though I had welcomed the brief interactions with the woman who hung on the threshold of death, tonight I had not come to bid her goodbye.

"It is my hope that in your passing, another soul will be ready to make the journey at last." My eyes drifted to the corner where a small form sat huddled, curled in on himself with nothing but a pair of dark eyes peering out from beneath dark bangs, the rest of his face hidden behind his knees.

Sun-hee too peered into the corner where my eyes had gone, straining to see the figure that was so plain to me but failing. While her presence at death's door made me visible to her, she did not have the sight to see the others.

"Won-shik?" she asked, assuming it was her late husband, standing and watching over her even from his death.

"No," I responded simply.

The old woman sighed with a weariness that went beyond her failing health. "My Jiwon."

I nodded solemnly. During his life, and even at the time of his death, Jiwon's aura had been as golden as Sun-hee's—the example of a life well lived, with honesty, integrity, and all things that helped one pass on to the Forever without issue. But a hesitation to leave and clinging on to the life force of someone who still lived had held him back, dimming his soul, so now it was like the sun hidden behind a dark storm cloud.

The boy had died too young and been unable to leave his mother's side. For sixty years, I had returned to this household in the hopes of urging Jiwon to make the final ascent but never with any luck.

"He refuses to leave your side," I explained.

The dark, wary eyes continued to watch me from the corner. Their constant vigil unceasing—unhindered by the aches and weariness of mortality.

"Oh, Jiwon. My boy . . . my boy." Sun-hee's hand stretched out from her pallet, reaching toward the corner in a beckoning way.

The spirit eyed me untrustingly before scurrying like a beetle over to where his mother's hand lay, palm up on the floor. Ghost fingers drifted over the pale flesh, and a smile drifted over Sun-hee's face, like she could feel the gentle caress.

"Don't let him stay here once I've gone," the elderly woman instructed me.

"That is what I hope to prevent," I assured her.

Jiwon and I stared each other down, the boy giving no indication one way or the other.

"Eomma, who are you speaking to?" Sun-hee's eldest daughter was in the doorway, clutching the frame timidly while peering into the darkened room.

"Death," Sun-hee rasped.

A sharp inhale of surprise came from the doorway, followed by a string of chants to ward off menacing spirits and my dark counterpart—mortality.

I rose from my place on the floor and moved to stand beside the dim spirit still trailing fingertips over Sun-hee's pale palm. I held my hand out to him in offering.

"Come, little one, it has been too long. It is time to follow her home."

Jiwon eyed me with trepidation, not moving.

Both of us looked as we heard it, that final rattle of life leaving Sun-hee. As the light went out of her body, her spirit only grew brighter, hovering over her old form for a moment, beckoning. Sun-hee's glow then passed through the ceiling and began the peaceful ascension to the Forever.

There were others in the room now, those of the living gathering around Sun-hee, weeping in grief as they checked her discarded body. I ignored them—the only one who was of my concern was the lost soul still cowering on the floor.

"She's gone now Jiwon. If you wish to remain with her, you need to leave this realm and follow her."

The boy looked around the room, studying the faces of his well-aged siblings and the children they'd begot. For the first time, I could see the awareness on his face, that he was not a part of the life they lived here.

Finally, he nodded and stood. Turning to me, Jiwon waited for my hand to stretch out and rest upon his cheek. Murmuring the age-old words given to me by the Creator, I watched the sun break free of the storm cloud as his shine returned.

"Go now." Shifting my hands into the deep sleeves of my robe, I watched the boy dissipate into nothing but his soul's glow and follow the path his mother had taken, up and out.

All around me, people mourned with tears and wailing. While it was a sorrowful sound, it was also a sweet refrain. Sun-hee had lived a long life, one which caused a great absence in the lives that had known her.

To be missed. To be remembered. What a miraculous thing that must be.

I liked to find the highest point in any city that I was in, block out the glow of its lights, and gaze up into the sky. If I looked hard enough and far enough, I could see past even the brightness of the stars to the soft blue glow of new souls descending and the warm golden hum of the experienced souls returning. It was a pleasant way to remind myself that I was connected to all of this in some small way, being the only one on earth to witness their arrival.

Once I'd had my fill of watching the burning souls travelling to and fro, I would return to the world at my feet. Searching for the names that called me, dim spirits of those trapped here in this realm and refusing to move on into their deep sleep or transition. Tonight however, I was not turning from the sky. Instead I wondered which of the bright lights drifting up might be Sun-hee and Jiwon. Mother and son, reunited at last. Sun-hee, who never forgot the child she had lost but found any opportunity to speak of the boy who had died after only nine short years of life. And Jiwon, who felt his mother's love for him so strongly, he hadn't been able to leave her side, even in death.

Humans were capable of such depths of emotion. It was something that I contemplated with interest and an inability to fully comprehend. I, who had no conscious memory of life because I had never made it that far, had never felt a bond created between myself and another living soul.

I sometimes felt fondness for those souls who I visited the most. The ones such as Jiwon, who clung onto their former lives and needed a great deal of coaxing before they were willing to let go. But that 'fondness' was not something that swept me away on a wave of sorrow in the moments of their final passing. Their connections were with the living they had left behind, not with me.

Perhaps there were some things that could only be understood through the act of living.

Tonight, the stars were alive with a bright shimmer, their gaseous essence competing with the travelling souls for most breathtaking. Did the Creator miss them when they left the Forever to journey down to earth and live their short human lives? Or did it bring great joy?

My gaze was captured by a particularly bright light falling through the dark heavens. This one descended with purpose, its final destination already chosen. As it drew closer, I could see it more clearly, how this one seemed to twinkle—a visual embodiment of laughter and glee. I smiled at the sight of it, and when the soul drifted closer to earth, falling in this same area of Wonju-mok, I was up on my feet to follow it.

Typically, I was not concerned with the beginning stages of life. Souls only became my priority if they refused to ascend when their time came. However, there was something in the twinkle that caught my attention and drew me forward. I found myself overcome with a need to know where the twinkling soul was going. Whose form would it choose? What family?

There was something special about the little twinkling soul, of that I was certain. Had the Creator sent someone wondrous to the earth who would change the lives of many? I wished to know.

The home was not large, but it was beautiful, owned by one of the jungin class—a government official and his young wife. They were asleep in their room, unsuspecting of the new life filtering down through the ceiling. Slipping beyond the walls from outside, I came to stand in the dark shadows of the corner. The twinkling soul hovered momentarily over the woman, as if acknowledging my presence, then sunk into her. For a moment, the woman's torso glowed with the faint blue twinkling light of the soul before all was dark in the room once more.

With nothing more to see, I found myself wandering

through the tiny home. Gazing at small, seemingly unimportant possessions that held some meaning or other for the couple. It was not much space for a growing family, but perhaps the laughter the new soul would bring to them would brighten the space up with all of that glee and light I had seen within it.

From across the globe, another lost soul called to me, ready at last to leave if I could only show them the way. Giving a final look around me, I left, following the call of one who needed me.

India

Sadvhi, a kind woman who had lived a hard but honest life, was recently deceased. Her body lay crumpled on the ground with the shadow of her angry husband standing over it still. Sadvhi panted, as if she were yet caught up in the struggle that had ended her life, the fear of it a catalyst for her having not begun her ascent.

She had lived a good life; I could see it in the warm glow about her. But her violent end was a strike of darkness that threatened to seep over her, darkening that shine with a dim cloud. If I were to feel sadness, it would be for these souls, who had lived a life of grace and thoughtfulness. Who should have had no issue in passing on but found themselves caught up in the injustice of their demise.

"Sadvhi," I called to her softly as I entered the home.

She did not stir at first, still caught up in watching her husband rush suddenly in an attempt to stop the flow of blood from the gash in her head. She had fallen, likely after a forceful shove, and her head had broken open on a nearby table. His actions were futile, as Sadvhi was already detached from her mortal flesh.

"Sadvhi." I spoke her name once more. This time, though startled, she turned to me.

It took a moment for recognition to dawn on her features, and when it did, her eyes filled with tears.

"Yamaraja," she rasped hoarsely. "You've come to rope me and carry me back to Yama-loka." She was fearful; I could see it in the flickering light of her soul.

"There will be no roping." I held my hand out to her, but she balked at the sight of it.

"I am not ready to be judged by you and the Yamadutas." Her gaze moved back to her husband, now hurrying to gather her body up in a sheet. It would seem that he had realized there was no saving his wife.

"Why do you fear it, Sadvhi?" She had lived a proper life; there was nothing to fear.

"I brought him to anger so many times. I fear where I will end up. What hell I will live through first before I may return here."

It was I that moved to her rather than the other way around. I took her hand, though it made her jump, and clasped it between my own. "You have nothing to fear. Sadvhi." I said her name so that she was forced to look at me. "The anger was all Aatish."

She did not believe me.

"I have come only to guide you on, not to punish you. You are meant to ascend to the Forever. Once you get there, if you wish to return to this world, you have only to ask the Creator." I reached out to cup her cheek. "Will you go?"

It was never a certainty. Many at this moment would hold onto their earthly concerns, believing that they had only darkness and pain to head on to. Instead of moving on, they would cling to this in-between afterlife. Preferring it to what they feared lay ahead.

I could not make the decision for Sadvhi.

Her gaze intent, she sought the answers in my own dark eyes. "I will go," she whispered at last.

Pleased, I nodded and murmured the words that would help cleanse the creeping shadow and allow her to let go. When she was ready, Sadvhi dissipated, and I watched her warmth rise up towards the vastness of the sky.

CHAPTER TWO
AN AMARYLLIS IN THE DARK

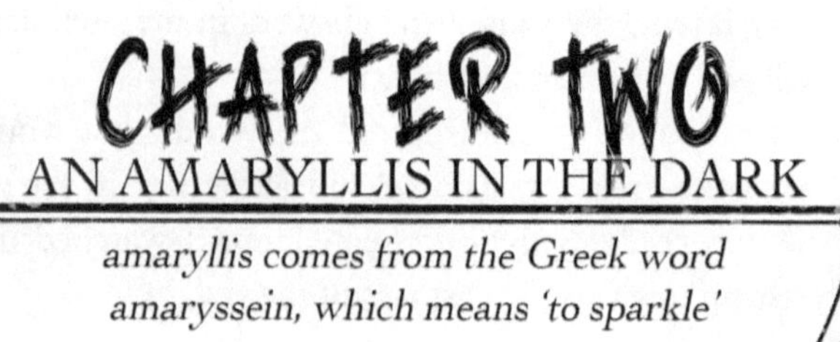

*amaryllis comes from the Greek word
amaryssein, which means 'to sparkle'*

Korea

I was not one to revisit the homes of the living, not unless they were on the edge of death and needed some final guidance. However, I found myself back in that small home on the edge of Wonju-mok the night the twinkling soul made their way into the world.

Nothing specifically told me that it would be happening. Like their creation, the birth of a new soul into the mortal realm is of no importance to me unless things go terribly wrong and I am required to direct the newly lost soul skyward. I was simply drawn to that part of the globe. Finding myself in the same corner of the room I had watched the soul enter its host for the first time.

The woman travailed throughout the night, and all the while I ignored the beckoning of souls needing my attention. I could not tear myself away from that birthing room until the wee hours of the morning when the cry of a newborn sounded out. When at last the squalling infant was placed upon her mother's chest, soothing a little at the warmth of her mother's skin pressed to her cheek, I allowed myself to fade away.

There were souls to collect, and a newly arrived one had no need of me.

I returned that night, however, standing over the couple's bed, the rosy-cheeked newborn nestled snuggly in the crook of her mother's arm. Gently, I reached out to brush phantom fingers over her forehead. Cream lids blinked open, and I was suddenly looking into a set of dark brown eyes that were clear and bright.

Her name was Bo-ah, meaning precious gem or treasure, and she gazed up at me as if she were able to see me. Then her eyes closed once more, and she slumbered.

Perplexed, I retreated. Removing myself back to one of my familiar rooftop perches to watch the sky.

Having never lived, I had no place among the living, no matter how those eyes may have looked up at me with acknowledgement.

"Hyun-woo."

The spirit shifted in his stance but refused to turn to look at me. Instead he remained facing a small bench that sat in the corner of the garden. Three weeks ago, the elderly soul had been teetering on the brink of being ready to enter the realm of slumber. Not a mortal who had lived well, he would not be going into the Forever and was hesitant to go on to his sleep. We had spoken when time allowed for it, and Hyun-woo's thoughts seemed to be aligning properly last I had visited.

Perhaps if I had been able to return sooner. Something had hindered his progression.

"You cannot ignore me, Hyun-woo." I drifted up alongside him, studying the bench he seemed so very focused on. "What happened?" I asked gently.

Still refusing to speak, he simply pointed to the garden wall. I gazed there, uncertain what could be so important about a garden wall that he would refuse to move on to his rightful resting place. My uncertainty turned to perplexity as I took note of a crack in the garden wall just large enough for the small child to be squirming her way through.

Her hanbok was a soft pink on the bottom and topped with a light yellow jacket. Both it and her hair had once upon a time been neatly presented. Now, however, the skirt of her hanbok was crumpled and bore a smudge, while her hair had been mussed by fingers, branches, or other means. Yet her appearance was no less precious for it. Cheeks rosy and rounded with a smile, her eyes shining with hope, she was a spark of light on this cloudy day.

Hyun-woo stirred at my side, moving forward to meet the girl at the bench in the garden. It was my great surprise to see the little girl greet the dimmed soul with a small bow and a pleased smile as she took her seat upon the bench, feet swinging in the air.

"Eomma said I wasn't to run off today, but I promised you. So here I am!" she chirped merrily.

Listening, I blinked in further surprise. She could see Hyun-woo...

Such a thing could not be possible. The young girl was not ill and near death, nor was her demise an accidental thing soon to happen. Beyond those who walked the threshold, I had never met a living soul who was able to see the dead.

It made me question everything that I knew and recognized as truth.

"Thank you," the elderly soul rasped, reaching out to pat the child's knee. "Did you find her?"

My eyes zeroed in on where Hyun-woo's hand had graced her knee. The dead could not make contact with the living, yet the action had been upon something solid. My mind buzzed.

The little girl nodded at his question, making a happy 'mhm' noise as she did so. Her feet swung a little faster from her perch on the edge of the stone bench, her hands clasping the edge of it to keep her from propelling forward.

Hyun-woo gazed down at her, a question in his eyes. The little girl smiled, her cheeks rounded and dimpling.

"And?" he pressed.

"I told her."

Listening, I frowned. This interaction should not be going on, and beyond the fact that it was, I didn't understand what was taking place between them. I longed to step forward and question Hyun-woo but had a feeling that he would not pay me any heed until he had his full answers from the child at his side.

He released a heavy breath, as if a great weight were escaping him. His shoulders sagged, and the dull shade of his aura lightened, just a little.

"She said I was an odd child and did not believe me at first," the little girl went on to explain. "I had to take her to the spot you told me about."

Hyun-woo's brow creased. "You took her to the boatyard?"

"You said he was buried there. She had to see, or she would not believe."

My frown deepened at these words. Slipping over the ground between them, I stopped before the old spirit.

"Hyun-woo," I said. "What is this about?"

I wasn't certain if he would choose to ignore me still or not. However, I was relieved to see that he was past his insolent phase and glanced up to me. There was a moment of surprise, as if he had forgotten my presence altogether, and then he nodded gravely. Answering a question that only he had heard.

"I am ready now," he responded.

Realizing that there were some things even I would not be given the answers to, I simply nodded. Hyun-woo stood from his bench, standing before me. Reaching out my hand, I placed it on his shoulder as I murmured the words that would put his soul to rest. Slowly, his eyes closed, and he began to fade out of sight.

When he was gone, his soul at last in the great sleep where his spirit could be cleansed of its ill, I turned my eyes upon the young girl, only to find her large brown eyes open and staring at me intently.

"You're not grey," she announced in confusion.

I paused in my actions, uncertain what was happening. Looking around, I made certain that there were no other souls around us before I looked back to the young girl who was staring up at me intently, waiting for me to respond.

"You can see me?" This was an impossible occurrence that should not be happening. I wasn't certain how to accept her dark brown eyes as they beheld me. I had never faced this situation before.

"Of course I can." She was so confident and assured. "But you're not like the others. Your soul isn't grey . . . it's blue." Her wide eyes blinked up at me. "Why?"

A heavy sigh left me, this question not something I had even pondered in all my years of existence.

"I suppose it is because I have not lived."

The little girl's head tipped to the side, further questions already building inside her young mind. "But I can see you. Where did you come from?"

This question, too, gave me pause. I had been wandering

the earth for so very long that it felt as if I had always just been. But I knew that I hadn't. That at some point, the Creator had nestled me in a warm, loving embrace and offered me this view of life rather than returning to the Forever without experiencing it at all.

"I believe. . . I was a babe that was not born," I explained, not wanting to get into dark details.

"How?"

"Sometimes, things simply happen."

The girl frowned a little. I reached out, unsure what would happen until my hand made solid contact with her head. Gently, I brushed a comforting hand down over her dark locks. It was an action I had witnessed many a parent perform on their child in an effort to soothe. I wasn't sure if I was doing it correctly.

The girl's eyes told me that she could tell I was acting out of assumption rather than experience. I drew my hand back to myself.

"Just like Hyun-woo leaving?"

"No," I stated. My head tipped to the side, realizing she may need more explanation than that. "Hyun-woo's passing on was long overdue."

"Then you should have helped him tell her what he needed her to know."

I looked down at her in surprise as she reprimanded me on this.

"The living cannot see me."

"I can."

Yes, she could. And I still felt myself reeling over this fact. It simply should not be. Had never been. "You are an abnormality."

She blinked up at me. "Why?"

"I do not know." And I truly did not. I had never seen one

of the living who were able to see me or the spirits that walked the earth around them. Not unless they were on the precipice of death. "Have you seen others? Besides Hyun-woo?"

The little girl nodded. "I see lots. Eomma says I shouldn't talk about them." Once again, her large brown eyes blinked up at me. "Do you think I shouldn't talk about them?"

This question seemed outside my knowledge, as I did not fully understand what it meant to be human or to live the lives they led.

"I believe little girls are meant to listen to their eommas."

She didn't seem precisely happy with this statement and sighed. Swinging her feet idly, her hands gripped onto the stone bench still, her eyes studying me. "Fine."

The proclamation made my lips twitch in a manner I wasn't accustomed to. There was something peculiar in the way she made the statement, as if she were older than what she was; a wise elderly woman adhering to the rule of lesser beings.

Another thought crossed my mind as I gazed down at the little girl before me. "Do you speak to all the spirits that you see?"

Most were harmless, but some of the grey spirits could become aggressive and angry once they had wandered the world too long. The ones whose anger became too fierce gained a corporeal essence to them that allowed them to connect with the physical world once more. This was the stage that I attempted to prevent the most. The living were not supposed to be aware of the dead.

"Not all of them . . ." Her words trailed off in a manner that made me suspicious.

"Are you sure?"

"They're angry because they can't speak to the ones they need to speak to!" she protested.

Feeling a sudden impulse to try and protect this child, I moved forward and knelt before her, bringing myself down to her level.

"The angry ones can become harmful to those who are living. You shouldn't speak to the angry ones."

"But who will help them?"

"I will."

She looked at me as if she did not believe what I was telling her.

"You didn't help Hyun-woo," she argued.

"I was helping him to move on before you arrived." I gazed at her. "I cannot speak to their families for them if that is what they wish. But I help them see that what they did or did not accomplish in life cannot change, and that death is meant to be accepted, and they must move on."

"But you didn't move on, you're still here."

"I never lived," I repeated, which made her frown.

"What are you?" Her small hand reached out to poke a finger into my arm, testing out once again that I was solid to her touch.

Her curiosity seemed to match my own over this moment, and I accepted the touch with a little amusement on my part. What did this child think of meeting a non-living soul who came for the dead?

"I have many names," I responded softly. "Most refer to me as Death."

"Jug-eum," she whispered solemnly, her eyes growing wide.

I only nodded.

"But that's not your name," she stated. Then she frowned. "Does Jug-eum have a name?"

"I am called Ephesus by the only one who sees fit to beckon me."

The Creator had not seen fit to beckon me in many rotations of the earth's passage.

The little girl smiled at me. "I am Bo-ah."

CHAPTER THREE
AN ALSTROEMERIA IN HAND

alstroemeria represent fortune, devotion,
and friendship

Ireland

I had discovered the twinkling soul once more.

It was not my place to interfere in the lives of the living or to have contact with them in any form, and up until this point, it had never been possible. I had known there was something special about the twinkling soul as I watched it drift down to earth to choose its host body, but this was not the expected outcome.

Once she had announced herself, I found myself shifting out of focus and leaving her behind in that small walled-in garden. Whatever the Creator intended for me, I did not believe it was colluding with the life of a young human. Instead, I travelled many countries away to be present at the side of a young teen who had fallen from a wall and was clinging to fragments of his life with a desperate but slipping grasp.

"It is okay to let go," I murmured to the boy, kneeling at his side.

His lids fluttered like frantic butterfly wings battling a

strong wind. A dusting of blood escaped his mouth on his exhale, coating the corner of his lips in crimson, and he tried to speak. It was there in the fading light of his eyes: fear.

"R-reaper," he rasped at last, eyes misting over.

Taking a seat on the rocky ground, I nodded at his statement. The boy shut his eyes as he drew in a shaky, wet breath, then exhaled another spray of red. The droplets clung to his lips as desperately as he did to life.

"I'm scared," he admitted at last.

Giving him another nod, I offered what I hoped was a comforting smile. "It is common, but unneeded. The Forever is not something to fear but to rejoice in."

He shook his head a little, as much as his broken body would allow. We were alone, and it would be hours before his empty frame was discovered by those who cared.

I could see the bright tint of his soul beginning to dim as he resisted the transition, fighting it in a mulish manner. If he did not accept his lot, he would be trapped here, wandering the rocky underside of this stone wall. I did not want that for him.

Reaching out a hand, I brushed my thumb across his forehead. "Niall, you mustn't resist it. Fighting will only trap you in an empty existence. It will not keep you in this life."

His light gaze only took on a more determined look, and I felt a weariness in my spirit, until the spot on his forehead where my thumb had brushed began to shimmer.

It was a rare occasion for those of his people who did not believe in its possibility, one that only happened with the most stubborn of souls who fought with a fierceness that could not be ignored. Niall was not going to remain in the Forever and he would not be fading into the deep sleep, the shimmer was a sure sign of it.

I began to smile at him in a brilliant manner that startled the dying boy laying sprawled on the ground. "You will return," I explained softly. "So do not fear. Release this body and travel into the vastness above. There will be another body, another life."

"Rebirth?" he whispered.

I nodded and watched happily as peace found its way into Niall's eyes before he closed them and let go of his broken body. His spirit, now a shimmering yellow, rose from his form. There was a smile on his translucent face, and no words were needed between us as he rose up into the vastness above us.

He would find his way back into the new form that was meant for him. Of that I was certain. Some simply clung so fiercely to who they were that they could not pass on to the Forever and remain there; a new life was all that would suffice for such souls.

Once I was sure he was gone, I stood, looking down at the steadily cooling frame he had discarded in his wake. Not for the first time I wondered what it was like to be inside one of those mortal shells. To feel the pain and the pleasure they were capable of. To understand what it was to be cold and to be hot. To hunger and thirst.

Humans were a strange lot. The world appeared to be filled with misery: pain, loss, illness, jealousy, and greed. Yet, people found a way to smile through it all. To seek out the people and events that would bring them joy, to such an extent that they very rarely wished to leave any of it behind.

There was very little in this world that drew me back to it.

Korea

The next time I was in that city of Wonju-mok, I found

myself overcome with curiosity and sought out the home of the twinkling soul, Bo-ah.

She was a little taller, but her cheeks still held the chubby swell of youth, and her eyes glowed with that same mixture of innocence and worldliness. She clung onto the childish belief in the impossible because she witnessed it every day.

When I found her, she was outside her home, drawing a picture in the soil with a stick. There was another small child with her who appeared more interested in chewing on the end of his stick than using it as an instrument of art.

Not wishing to interfere, I remained in the shadows. There was no worry of the youngest child noticing me, or anyone else on the street for that matter. It was Bo-ah I did not wish to interrupt. Instead, I watched, taking note of her interactions with the younger child. How she kept a watchful eye on him, reaching out to pull bits of bark from between his lips whenever he managed to gnaw a piece off.

Seeing there truly wasn't anything remarkable in the ways of children, I prepared to leave, sensing the presence of another spirit on the verge of transitioning. But I was stopped as a trio of children came upon Bo-ah and her stick-chewing companion.

The change in Bo-ah was subtle but evident. Her shoulders tensed as she sensed their approach, and it made me frown in curiosity. She hadn't acted in such a way around Hyun-woo, or even myself. So why did other children bring out an instinctive discomfort in her?

"Look, it's Mad-One digging in the soil," one little boy declared. The toe of his jipsin dug at her lines, marring them.

Bo-ah's shoulders stiffened, and I watched, head tipping to the side, as a muscle twitched in her jaw.

"What are you doing, Mad-One? Telling all your ghosties how to find you? Or trying to ward them off?" He brought his fingers up before him, making a sign with them as if warding off an evil spirit.

Bo-ah had yet to say anything in response, her dark, round eyes saying all that needed to be said. An anger brewing in their depths had chased away the typical light.

Spurred on by the tallest boy, another at his side reached out to shove at Bo-ah's shoulder, causing her to stumble back a little. The anger in her eyes only grew colder, though she remained silent still.

I frowned in displeasure watching this behaviour. Such violence in ones so young was not a pleasant thing to see. I also did not appreciate the attack on my twinkling spirit. Her happiness and light were something that should not be diminished.

"Nothing to say? But you speak so much to your spirits. Have they stolen your ability to talk to people?" The tallest boy clapped his hands mere inches from her face.

I made a motion to step from the shadows, then paused. My presence would go entirely unnoticed. The only one who would see would be Bo-ah, and I sensed that in this situation, the presence of a ghostly spirit would not help her. Instead, I continued to take in this strange occurrence. Were children typically so volatile towards each other? Was it something that came naturally to them, or was it learned? The spirits that fell from the Forever to drift into awaiting forms did not come violent and cruel, of that I was certain. Did the body they entered make them so? Tainted by the parents who had created it?

Or was it life on this earth, growing up in their surroundings and suffering, that brought about this sort of behaviour? Perhaps all children held a certain amount of darkness within them, a darkness they either chose to embrace or to discard as they grew.

"Bo-ah?" the little boy called, pulling his stick from his mouth long enough to utter it.

I watched her eyes shift to the small child momentarily. The hand at her side motioned for him to be silent, and then her attention returned to the three before her once more. The little boy seemed to contemplate whether to listen to her silent urgings or speak again. In the end, he returned to his stick.

The third child, who up until this moment had remained silent, seemed to find his own place in the jeering and stepped forward. He grabbed the stick quickly from her hand and then smacked her with it.

The sound of the stick swished through the air before slapping at her fleshy cheek with a sharp noise. It made me startle. I had witnessed many vicious behaviours in mortals over my time surveying the world, but it had been the hatred of adults. Their jealousy and greed. Their tendency to tumble into self-destructive habits.

I had believed children were innocent. Free from the darknesses of adulthood.

I found myself wishing that I could take that stick and swat the three boys with it in return, let them feel whatever it was Bo-ah had felt.

From the shadows, I glided into the street proper, no longer able to stay hidden. From the corner of her eye, Bo-ah took note of my presence, and something in her countenance changed.

Raising her hands curled like the angry paws of a tiger before her, she bared her teeth and released a loud, screeching howl. Rushing towards the boys, it was enough to startle them and send them stumbling backward. Seeing the effectiveness of it, Bo-ah let loose with another howl and rushed them once more.

"Demon!" the shortest one shouted, spinning on his heel

to race away. He didn't stop to see if the other two were coming or not. They were. Following quickly at his heels, the boys ran down the street, disappearing around a corner.

Bo-ah's hands dropped to her sides once they were out of view, and then she turned slowly to me. There was an emotion in her gaze that I could not quite place; something wise and terribly youthful all at once.

Suddenly, she smiled, bowing quickly. She then looked up at me, the red welt from her lashing standing out on the rounded curve of her cheek. "You've come back!"

"Yes," I replied. "Are those boys always so cruel?"

She shrugged a little at my question, stooping down to pick up her stick so that she could poke absently at the ground with it.

"What did you do to bring it upon yourself?"

This time, my question brought back that flash of anger I had seen before. However, quickly enough, it was gone and replaced with her light. "They think I am strange because I can speak with spirits."

"But mortals pray and speak to the past spirits of their ancestors all the time. Why should what you can do seem so strange to them?"

Bo-ah gave me a measured look, one that said I was naive in the ways of humans.

"They speak without seeing."

"Bo-ah?" It was the small boy. His wet stick now hung at his side as he ventured forward to stand beside her. He looked around us, confused. "Who are you talking to?"

Bo-ah smiled down at him, patting the top of his head. "Just the wind, Ha-ru." From beneath her lashes, she peered up at me, smiling secretively.

Understanding what was behind the moment, I only nodded to the girl before fading away.

CHAPTER FOUR
A PATCH OF BRIAR

the meaning of sweet briar is to be wounded

France

The field before me lay strewn with bodies. Some writhed and groaned in agony, while others grew steadily colder. As I wandered over the ground drenched in blood, I watched men continue to face off against each other. The clang of swords echoed in the early morning air. This was a battle I had been watching for nearly ten decades. The battlefield changed, so too did the victory—falling to one side or the other as the years passed. Valiant heroes came and went.

The one thing that did not change was the death.

Some met their end fearlessly, believing in their fight until their final breath with a single-minded purpose that transitioned them into the Forever with no hesitation or regrets. Then there were the others, so many others, forced into a war for the purpose of those in power, dragged from their homes without a say. These entered death with fear and laminations and so many unfinished desires.

The dim souls left wandering the desolated fields or ruins

of demolished cities in the wake of battle were difficult to number. Some could be ushered into acceptance, but most clung to the hope of making their way home without ever being able to find their way off the field of their demise.

If hatred was a thing I understood, I felt it for this beast known as war. So much loss for the sake of the vanity of two countries, furious kings whose greed and ego led only to death of their subjects. I was certain this was not the purpose of life, not what the Creator had meant for the mortal lives sent down to experience it all.

Yet they tore themselves apart over foolish squabbles.

I felt a tug at the end of my robe, and looking down, found a hand clutching onto it and a pair of light blue eyes gazing up at me through a veil of blood. A large gash in the side of his head had torn away his blond hair and caused a river of red to flow freely from him, soaking into the mud below.

"Saint Joseph . . . is that you?" he rasped through dry lips. Licking at them, he released a shuddering breath.

Kneeling beside him, my fingers gently brushed through his soaked hair, picking loose strands from his eyes. He was so very young to be returning to the Creator, a life barely lived. I felt disgust for these things known as captains and commanders, leading their men, old and young, to such wasted deaths.

"Are you here . . . to lead me home?" His skin was turning a light shade of grey, the light in his eyes dimming. They were filled with uncertainty and fear. "Will it hurt?"

I offered what I hoped was a consoling smile and pressed a hand to his cheek. His eyes shut for a moment, and the soldier leaned into the touch. When his eyes opened once more, I shook my head. "Fear not, Pierre. You will be welcomed with loving arms. Go to it in peace."

He smiled briefly, some of the fear slipping away, before

he closed his eyes and drifted away. I waited until I was sure his bright glowing spirit had left unhindered, then I returned to my progress across the field.

I was stopped once again when I found a young soul, his golden glint dimmed by grey and his arm clutched to his chest with his opposite hand. He seemed to be searching the ground, frantically looking for something.

"Charles," I called softly.

He glanced up to me for but a moment, and then his eyes returned to the field. His steps were erratic, shifting him from one spot to the next in quick succession. "Have you seen my hand? I'm trying to find my hand."

Souls did not have missing limbs. Despite what happened to the mortal flesh in death, it did not carry over to the eternal spirit. However, memories, especially traumatically painful or terrifying ones, left their marks. Across the field, I could see young Charles' body laying handless and speared through with the broken shaft of an arrow.

"You've not lost it, Charles, look down at your arm. It is there," I soothed, moving forward.

However, the soul remained unhearing. I tried reaching out to rest my hand on his shoulder in hopes of clearing away some of the greying shadow, but he reacted violently. Both arms rose up before him, lashing out at me in protest as he wrenched backward. He panted in a haggard manner, even though breath was no longer needed for him.

"I've got to find my hand!" he screeched at me, whirling away. "They've taken my hand!"

Looking on in sadness, I left him to his wandering. The wounds were too fresh, his death too sudden. It may take decades for his soul to accept the fact that he was indeed dead. Until then, he would wander this field in search of himself. I would keep an eye on him in hopes he did not become a gallu, one of the truly violent corporeal spirits that could manifest harm on the mortal world. But until he was ready, he would not hear.

As the battle finally wound to a close, and both sides withdrew to their respective camps, dragging with them the bodies of the dead and wounded, I continued my journey through the spirits left behind. Helping those who were ready but hesitant and convincing a few of the dimmed souls that they had nothing to remain here for.

However, there were far more left on the field than pleased me. Watching their dark presence wander lost and lonely, oblivious even to each other, I wondered what battle had actually been won here today. For I certainly could see what had been lost.

I could yet feel the draw of one soul who was perhaps not so far into the grey that they could not be saved, and so I made my way into one of the campaign tents, set up on the outskirts of the field. The gentle drift of smoke from chimneys in the next city dotted the sky just over the hill beyond it.

Inside the tent, a group of men stood round a table, peering down at a piece of parchment held down with pots of ink and arrowheads.

"Tomorrow, we take Les Tourelles and Les Augustins. Once we've gained control of the gatehouse, the infantry can make camp there, and the wounded can be housed at the convent," a stern man in refined garments proclaimed.

My attention wasn't on him, or on the men heeding his commands, but on the spirit who hovered beside him, gazing down at the parchment with a keen set of eyes and nodding.

"What was our body count for today?" the spirit asked. When no one responded to him, he asked once more, looking at each face around him in turn.

"Edward," I said gently.

Though he did not turn at once, I noticed the way his form stilled. He had heard my call.

"Edward, you are dead."

Slowly, the soul turned to peer over at me, his grey glow faint. It was his sense of duty that kept him here, standing in this tent, overseeing what would be the preparations for further battle.

"Dead?" he asked, hesitation in the way he sounded out the single syllable, almost making it two.

I nodded solemnly, gazing at him. He eyed me curiously, head tipped slightly at an angle.

"Do all angels look like you?"

"I am not an angel," I responded.

He seemed relieved at this. "Is Death a demon then? Is that why your skin is dark?"

I wondered if my face bore a look of confusion. "I have no skin, just as you do not."

Did he see me like the people of my homeland? Or the place, at least, where I was meant to be born? Most perceived me in the role of death that was most familiar to them, calling me by the name of that figurehead. As a slim male with darkly tanned skin and a swatch of dark, curly hair, I was rarely what they thought their spirit of death would look like. A comment that was frequently made.

Edward Burgess frowned more deeply as he gazed at me, and I saw the way his soul light dimmed a little more. I understood he was not meant for the Forever. Not yet. His destination was the deep sleep.

"Are you to usher me off? I thought angels were meant to take us on to heaven."

"I only help bring you to acceptance. You find your way there on your own."

He looked back at the gathering of men around the table, and I watched his shoulders sag out of their rigid formation.

"They truly cannot hear me?" He did not seem entirely convinced. Reaching out, he waved a hand before the face of one of the men, only to drop it back down at his side when it drew no reaction. "Well, let us move on with it then."

Edward turned to face me with an expectant look. Without hesitation, I stepped up to him, placing my hand on his shoulder as I murmured, sending him into the plane of deep slumber.

When he was gone, I turned back to the open field and gazed on the lost souls. I felt empty within myself. Days of ceaseless wandering stretched out before me. Only the living finally came to an end.

Korea

I should not have returned to Wonju-mok, but there was no expectation or duty in our conversations. And I found myself curious still.

It was the need of a grey soul that called me to each new place, and I found them without even seeming to try. It was different when searching for the twinkling soul. Another part of me had to search, a piece that had to stretch out over the city. A part of me that enjoyed the searching as much as the finding, for it was a break from the normality of my days and the ease of my own shifting from one location to the next.

This time when I found Bo-ah, she was seated beneath a tree, plucking the petals off a blossom and watching them float away on the breeze. I hesitated only a moment before gliding over to her. Unlike last time, she noticed my presence right away. Looking up, she smiled and patted the grass beside her.

I eyed the ground for a moment, pondering my choices, and then sat down, folding my legs beneath me.

"You weren't gone as long this time," she stated, an impish grin tugging her lips upward. "Did you miss me?"

My head tipped sideways as I surveyed her. Had I missed her? "I don't believe I know that feeling."

Bo-ah blinked up at me, her fingers stilling on the final petals.

"When you miss someone, you sort of hurt . . . in here." She reached over to tap the centre of my chest. "There can be an empty hole shaped like them inside you."

"I do not have an empty hole shaped like you," I explained, finding this idea rather preposterous.

She shrugged, not seeming overly concerned whether I did or not.

"Why are you plucking petals?" I questioned.

"They're soft." She picked up one of the blossoms from her lap and held it out to me.

"I won't be able to touch it."

"What?" She looked surprised.

To show her, I reached out and tried to pick up a nearby petal from the ground, letting her see how my fingers passed through it without connecting.

"But I can touch you." Her finger slipped into my hand, a seemingly frail thing but with evident strength.

I thought about this for a moment before responding. "I can touch those on the brink of death when they're able to see me. You must somehow walk the line between planes."

Bo-ah simply nodded, accepting this explanation with little resistance. She plucked another petal. Resting it on her open palm, she held her hand in the air and waited until the breeze caught it. Together, we watched it dance in the air before us, then flutter away.

"Where do you go when you're not here?" she asked me.

"Wherever I am needed."

"Needed for what?" Her flowers were forgotten once more, her wide brown eyes upon me instead.

"Helping souls return as I did Hyun-woo."

"Return where?"

I blinked at her. "You have a lot of questions."

Bo-ah simply smiled and nodded. "Return where?" she repeated.

"The Forever, where all souls come from."

She contemplated this for a little while. "When we die, we go back there."

"Yes."

"But not you?" I merely shook my head at this question, and so she continued. "But did you come from the Forever?"

"I believe so."

"Then why don't you get to go back there?" She was frowning a little.

"The Creator needs me here. Helping."

I hadn't really considered it an option before, my returning to the Forever. If I had gone back, rather than staying here on earth watching over the dim souls, would I have been able to return? Been reborn to another life? Or would that have been the end of it for me?

"Well, I'm glad you didn't go back." She smiled at me and reached out to take my hand once more, holding it in her tiny one. "You can come talk to me whenever you like."

CHAPTER FIVE
AN AMARANTHUS DROPPED

amaranthus caudatus is the flower of
hopelessness and heartbreak

The days had lengthened, and the trees bloomed to full brilliance. While I could not smell the sweetness on the breeze or feel the warmth of the sun on my face, I could appreciate the beauty. The process the world cycled through, mimicking the lives of humans with its growth, height of beauty and then eventual fading until death took hold, had always intrigued me. While the humans referred to it as seasons, I saw the way their own lives would play out.

Bo-ah was still in the spring of her life, a sapling stretching for every ray of sunshine that she could absorb. However, the beings around her that she called friends were mostly those who'd already passed into the winter of theirs. Even I recognized this as not something that was typical for children.

I came across her in the market, and though she took note of my presence, she did not acknowledge me beyond a subtle smile in my direction. Noting the very populated area, I remained quiet, following along behind her with my hands clasped at my back.

She handled purchasing from the vendors with a maturity that seemed beyond her years, and I watched in fascination. There was a sort of banter that went on back and forth between them. While I would have anticipated her paying whatever was asked, it would seem her mother had given her a set amount not to go past for each item, and Bo-ah would not be deterred.

When at last she was walking away from the market, I moved up alongside her. "You negotiate very well."

"Eomma made me recite what each was worth and said I was not to pay any more than what she told me." Her dark brown eyes glanced up at me. "They think because I am young I don't know. But I do."

There was pride in her eyes at this accomplishment.

"Are you headed home?" I asked, easily following along with her short gait.

"Yes, Eomma said I had to return with these items before I was allowed to go visit—" Her words halted, and she bit at her bottom lip as if to stem the tide of words.

"Go visit who?"

"A friend," came her weak reply.

I peered down at her face more closely. She was not one to speak with a timid or quiet nature, so I did not trust this behaviour from her now. "Do you not wish to tell me?" She shook her head a little. "Why?"

"Because you'll make them leave as you did Hyun-woo."

"Your friend is one of the dimmed," I stated.

Bo-ah nodded, her fingers clutching onto the fabric bag slung over her body.

"They are not meant to remain."

"I *know*. But they're happy as they are, and they do not wish to leave!" she protested.

I paused in my gliding beside her, and it forced Bo-ah to

stop as well. I waited until she had turned to face me, looking a little ashen in the face.

"Each soul only gets so much time allotted to them. When that time is over, they are meant to return to the Forever." I strove for a voice that was stern. Or, what I imagined stern sounded like.

"I know that too," she grumbled. "But she's my friend, and she's not ready. She's afraid."

"Afraid of what?"

"Of where she will go!" Bo-ah seemed upset, which was unlike her.

I looked at her more closely, wondering if it was only the fear of the unknown that bothered her. "It is a wonderful place. There is nothing to fear."

Bo-ah toed at the earth with her woven jipsin, avoiding eye contact with me. I was getting the sense that there was more to what she wasn't saying than what she was.

"Bo-ah?" I pressed once more.

"I don't want her to go." Her eyes, when they peered up at me, were wide and sorrowful.

I had seen what the living children could be like with her, and wondered if that was generally the behaviour towards her.

"Living children aren't meant to be friends with dim souls."

"Then why can I see them?!" It wasn't like her to raise her voice, and her tone seemed to have surprised even her, for once her words had echoed in the air around us, she stepped back a little, biting at her lip.

I paused, for her question had merit. Why *had* the Creator given her these abilities?

"Perhaps you are meant to do what I cannot do," I mused. I reached out a hand and placed it atop her head. It was warm from the sun, and I felt the heat tingle along my palm.

"You can share their concerns with those still alive, whereas I cannot. You eased something within Hyun-woo that I was unable to and helped him to move on."

I could almost see these thoughts mulling around in her mind as she considered this.

"Do you think so?"

I barely understood why the Creator had chosen to leave me here on earth in the role that I fulfilled. Whether Bo-ah had been purposefully gifted with this ability, I did not know. But it seemed unlikely that it should happen unintentionally.

"I do," I said at last.

This caused her to smile softly, and her form eased a little. "Do you want to meet her?"

I felt surprise go through me at this offer. I had not anticipated her being willing to take me to the friend she did not want to lose.

"I do."

"Okay. These items to my eomma first, then I will take you to meet Sulli."

Our progress down the street commenced once again, and a comfortable silence fell between us. Though I couldn't be sure, I thought perhaps Bo-ah was busy thinking on her purpose and why she had been gifted as she was.

I let her have the time and remained quiet. Silence was not something that bothered me but was rather a peaceful state to be in. Too often the world was full of clatter that only distracted from the true importance of the moment.

Humans were so easily drawn away from where they were meant to be and caught up in the noise of the chaos instead.

While Bo-ah hurried into her family home, I waited outside, gazing up at the large flowering tree outside the Yeo household. The blossoms rustled lightly in the breeze, and I noticed one break free of its perch and float down. Lifting my hand as if to catch it, I watched it pass through my palm on its way to the ground.

"Yeo Bo-ah, you be home in time to eat with your family!" a voice called out from behind me.

I turned to watch Bo-ah come running towards me.

"Yes, Eomma!" Bo-ah called back, skidding to a stop beside me. "Come! She hasn't given me much time."

The young girl wasted no time in heading back down the street. Her jipsins slapped lightly on stone as she ran, the loose strands of her dark hair catching in the wind. I followed easily.

She did not look back at me as she turned down an alley and raced to the end of it, coming out on another street. There was an eagerness in her steps which remained until she fetched up on the side of a stone bridge. I thought perhaps she had stumbled, then realized she had meant to do that.

Climbing up onto it a little, her hands clutching the top, she called out, "Sulli! Cho Sulli! I am here."

I remained at the end of the bridge, not stepping onto it. If a dim spirit was not ready to speak with me, my presence was often displeasing, and I did not wish to scare Bo-ah's friend away.

For a moment, nothing happened. And then a spirit appeared. She looked to be prepubescent. In life, she had been on the cusp of becoming a young woman but had not quite made it. I wondered if it had been an illness that had taken her.

There was a warmth beneath her grey clouds, one that told me she was not someone meant to go into the deep sleep but should have passed into the Forever without issue. I wanted to ask what had kept her here but remained silent. There was enough grey to her spirit for me to recognize someone who was not ready to be approached by me yet.

"Bo-ah, I thought you would be here sooner," the spirit scolded softly, though there was a smile of happiness on her lips.

"I'm sorry, my friend arrived, and I had to talk to him first."

"Your friend?"

Bo-ah glanced over her shoulder in my direction, and Sulli's eyes followed. She balked at the sight of me, her essence threatening to flicker away.

"Wait!" Bo-ah cried. "Don't go! He means you no harm. He's only here to talk."

Sulli's face darkened, an almost sinister cloud shrouding it. "Jug-eum does not come merely to speak. You know I am not ready!" She looked at Bo-ah accusingly.

"He prefers to be called Ephesus, and he knows you are my friend. He won't make you go." She turned to me. "Right? You won't make her go?"

My gaze shifted between the living and the dead girl, then, slowly, I shook my head. "I cannot make anyone go who does not choose to." I moved closer on the bridge, hoping to do so in a way that made me appear less threatening to her.

"I don't believe you." She looked at Bo-ah once more. "You know we haven't found them yet. They still don't know. I can't go yet!"

Fearful of my presence, Cho Sulli disappeared, preferring to hide rather than risk it.

Bo-ah sighed and slumped against the railing of the bridge.

"Who needs to be told what?" I asked, slipping up beside her now that Sulli was gone.

Bo-ah looked up at me sadly. "Her parents. That she didn't jump. She fell."

My eyes drifted down to the water below, and I nodded

in understanding. "Bring me back when she's ready to speak to me. Until then, I will stay away."

France

I was on the same battlefield. The fighting had moved into other parts of the city and beyond, only to end up on the same field. This time with the formerly defeated claiming victory.

The death was still the same, whomever held the white flag of defeat. Blood-soaked earth spoke only of loss, the scarlet essence of enemy and foe blending into one pool that was indistinguishable.

I moved from one dying form to another, doing my best to encourage acceptance before the shadow could pass over their spirits.

While the Creator had not spoken to me in a very long time, I could feel the sadness that hung thick over this battlefield. Humans had freedom of will to do as they pleased with their lives, but killing was not something the Creator had ever intended for mortal lives. Yet they could not seem to stop themselves.

Spotting a man lying on top of another, a sword thrust through his chest and blood trickling from his lips, I stepped up to him. Kneeling down, I found a pair of hazel eyes looking up into mine. He coughed, and I heard the gurgle of blood deep in his lungs.

"Are you one of that witch's demons come to steal my soul?" he rasped. Another cough raked through his body, and he winced as it shifted the sword.

"I do not collect, merely usher on." I knelt, wiping the droplets of blood from his lips with the sleeve of my robe. I felt sadness for the sudden tragic waste of life. Such a precious thing that I couldn't touch but which had been stolen so soon from another.

He took a shallow breath, eyeing me. "Usher me where?"

There was a blue shade to his spirit that hovered just above his body. "To the deep sleep."

"Will the witch follow me there?" he asked, concern flaring in his eyes.

"No. No one will follow you into your sleep."

I gazed around the field, then looked to him once more.

"Good," he whispered.

"Who is the witch?" I questioned in turn.

"She's bewitched them all," he rasped. "They sold their souls for an ungodly victory."

This time, his coughing ended only when his body gave up. His spirit hovered for a moment, hazel eyes firm on my face. "To sleep?"

"To sleep."

He did not need my help; there was acceptance within him knowing that the 'witch' would not follow, and so he faded out of this realm into the next.

How many more of them would be hesitant to transition, believing some unholy creature had stolen their lives away? I felt the sadness of my Creator within myself. More than just lives had been lost here today.

CHAPTER SIX
SNAPDRAGONS TORN ASUNDER

a symbol of strength, snapdragons are also a
charm against lies

Kenya

A body rested propped up against a tree, the sprawling branches overhead acting like an umbrella of protection from the night sky. A slick coat of blood glistened on her thighs, and a dark, twisted cord trailed up over her stomach to the infant squirming in her arms, its tiny fist flailing lightly. For the moment, the infant was silent, but it would not be long before hunger or cold caused it to cry out and signal to all the creatures lurking in the dark that it was alone.

Jira stood a few feet away, gazing down at the body that had once been her own, a dark storm cloud covering her spirit. As I approached, I watched her move to kneel down beside her body, fingers brushing lightly over the head of the infant, and then rise to pace around the tree. Her eyes shifted to the landscape around her, searching for threats on the darkening horizon.

When her eyes fell on me, Jira froze.

"Are you the great chameleon, or the lizard?" she whispered, dark eyes narrowing in suspicion.

"I suppose you can think of me as the lizard," I responded, coming to stand before her.

The myths of her people said that God had sent the great chameleon to inform man they would never die, but the chameleon was followed by the great lizard, who told them that they would.

Jira hissed and looked back down at the infant and her abandoned body. "Why have you come? It is my right to watch over my child."

I folded my hands behind my back, surveying the scene. "Staying won't provide you the comfort you believe it will. She will not be able to speak with you as is believed."

Though, the twinkling spirit had managed it; perhaps there were more capable of communing with the dead than I had believed. There were so many things I wished to ask the Creator, if only I were to be given the chance.

Jira shook her head in denial. "There are those who remember me. I will not be forgotten. They will help her to know, to remember too. I can stay and watch over her." She had turned and was now peering down at the infant. Her lids fluttered open, and she gazed up, almost as if seeing her mother's spirit standing there above her. "Had I known that she would arrive tonight, I would not have come this way . . . I would not have been alone when the pains started."

Her voice drifted off, and I wondered if she thought of her dying here on the ground, torn asunder by bringing her child into the world and fading away so that she could live.

"You can watch, but you will not be able to affect change. Your influence over the living realm has ended."

Jira shook her head, and I sighed. The eyes she turned on me were fierce and afraid. "I cannot leave her, they will smell the blood soon." I could see her straining, as if listening for the sounds of their manic laugh on the winds. The hungry hyenas who would come for the remains.

If only I were able to signal to those in the world of the living. Was it jealousy I was feeling for Bo-ah's ability to speak to both the living and the dead?

"Will any come looking for you? Were there those who knew where you had gone?"

Abandoned beside her body was a clay urn, the earth below it wet from where the water had spilled out.

"Dume will come. He will know." She seemed certain of this.

"Then we shall wait until then."

There would be no convincing this mother to leave behind her young before she was certain that she was safe, and I couldn't say that it was my desire to try.

Standing beside Jira, I could sense the anxiety radiating off her. It caused the darkness of her cloud to swirl around her more intensely. If Dume did not arrive, and the hyenas came instead, Jira would be at risk of becoming a gallu, I was certain of it.

"You should be prepared—"

"No," she interrupted me. "Dume will come, and he will find our daughter. There is still time." Her voice was firm, unyielding. She would not allow herself to think otherwise, at least not out loud.

The grey still swirled violently through her, choking out the golden hue of her soul, darkening it until I grew more concerned.

"Do you have a name for her?" I asked, seeking to take her mind off the threats in the darkness.

"I would have named her Kanoni," she murmured softly, tenderness wrapped up in that name.

"Little bird," I stated, mulling it over as I peered down at the newborn. "Fitting."

"She will soar on wings of strength. Perhaps the chameleon will bring her everlasting life."

I remained silent, allowing her to keep her hopes and desires for the life she had brought into the world.

"Are spirits of the sky capable of understanding love?" Jira asked me, breaking the silence that lay between us.

"I see it," I responded.

"But you do not feel it."

I thought about this. "No. I do not think so." Except perhaps the affection I felt for my souls . . . Was that love?

Jira's hand pressed to her chest. "Love is an all-consuming emotion. I would give all that I am to see her safe and happy. She is the essence of my world, living outside of myself."

I did not know this feeling, of that I was sure: my self, wrapped up entirely in the life of another.

My eyes drifted to the stars, and I wondered if the Creator was watching us now. If I asked, would help be sent that would protect Jira's infant from the wilds around us? Protect the essence of her world?

The only answer to my question was a high-pitched call in the distance that ended in an eerie laugh-like bark. Jira turned quickly in the direction of the sound, fear rising off of her in waves. It would seem time was running out.

"He will come, he must come," she chanted. Suddenly, she turned on me, grabbing fistfuls of my robe. She pulled me closer to her, features pinched with desperation. "Please, *do* something! Are you not connected to the great one in the sky? Ask that Dume be sent!"

The close proximity made me wish to back up, but I remained where I was, giving her the comfort of the force she could exert on me. The only option open to her at the moment.

"I cannot."

"*Why?* You brought death to us, why can you not hold it

back? Call the chameleon here to bring life. Just for now . . . just for now!"

I wished that there were a way I could bring her the relief that she sought, but life and death were out of my hands. I was only an observer, here to help ease people into acceptance. I had no control.

Over anything.

The eerie barking-laughter intensified as the creatures drew nearer. It would not be long now as the scent of blood led the way.

Jira pushed away from me, her spirit moving to kneel beside her body, arching over her daughter in an attempt to shield her.

I thought of Bo-ah and her desire to pass on the words and regrets of the past. Taking their last desires to those still living. A plea arose within me, one that I did not fully understand, and my eyes lifted once more to the stars above us. *Don't let this child die.*

This time, as the call of the hyenas sounded out, so too did a cry of concern.

"Jira! Jira, are you there?"

From out of the trees, a small hunting party carrying torches and spears appeared. The light flickered off their worried features, dancing over high grasses that swayed in the breeze. At her name, Jira's head lifted, and she looked to the searching group.

"Dume!" she called back. "I'm here! I'm right here!"

Standing, Jira lifted her hands in the air, calling out more frantically.

Her calls made no sounds to the living. Unless the babe decided to complain, the group would pass them by in the night.

Jira continued to call out to them, desperate for their recognition. I instead turned my attention to the infant.

Kneeling down beside her, I reached out to press my hand against her cheek. So full of life. I made no contact, but even still, her eyes opened, and I felt the connection.

"Cry, little one," I whispered. "Cry for your father to find you."

The baby only blinked at me.

I felt the plea rise up once more, a silent call for help. Life was not fair, and longevity was promised to no one. But even still, I desired for this one to be given a fighting chance.

The infant blinked up at me once more, and then her tiny face scrunched up in protest, and she released an angry cry into the air above her.

It was enough to capture the attention of the hunters.

Stepping back, I watched as the party came upon Jira's form. Dume sank to his knees before his family, wails of sorrow releasing from him as he bundled them into his arms.

Jira watched on, her own expression pained. Taking her elbow, I pulled her back from the sight.

"She is safe now," I reassured.

"Let me stay. Let me watch over her." Jira turned to look at me, her eyes pleading.

Gently, I shook my head. "Remaining does not bring peace. It brings longing and sorrow as you watch those you love grow and move on. The dead are not meant to watch the living. They are meant to return to the sky."

"Just a little while longer."

We watched and waited, until Dume and his small band of warriors had wrapped the child in a spare skin and lifted Jira's body beneath her shoulders and her ankles. Carefully, they carried her away, disappearing beyond the trees.

Korea

Bo-ah was seated in the branch of the tall tree outside the Yeo family home when I arrived, having sought her presence in the streets of Wonju-mok. While there were many souls out there I could seek out to answer my question, it was the twinkling soul I most wanted to hear from.

She didn't notice me until I was beneath her, her dangling feet level with my eyes.

"Ephesus!" she called my name, a smile upon her lips as she finally spotted me.

"Hello."

"How are you?" she asked, still grinning.

Head tilting to the side, I gazed at her. I didn't understand the question. "I don't change."

Bo-ah snickered. "But that doesn't mean you always have a good day. Are you happy?"

Happiness was another emotion I did not fully comprehend. I saw the way people smiled at each other. I heard their laughter when something truly delighted or amused them. I listened to them declare their happiness time and time again. People, possessions, gifts, surprises . . . these were just some of the things that seemed to bring joy to mortals. But just as my days did not change, new things did not come along to usher in this emotion.

"I am curious," I answered instead.

Her head tipped sideways as she peered down at me. "About what?"

"Love."

Bo-ah's brows shot up, and then she giggled. "Do you liii-iike someone?" she asked, giggling more.

This question only caused more curiosity to mount within me. "What is your definition of like?"

Still giggling, the little girl slid down out of the tree, landing before me with a soft thump. Taking my hand, she pulled me into the garden at the side of the house. Beneath one of the trees sat a little bench that she drew me to.

Once we were seated on it, she gazed up at me, a serious look on her face. "My eomma and appa like each other. So they got married and now have a family together," she explained.

I nodded, understanding a little. "When one feels love or like for another, they choose to join together?"

"Well, I love my little brother, but I didn't choose to be with him. I just have to be because we live in the same place."

I remembered the stick chewing child and wondered if that was her brother.

"So love does not always mean you live in the same place?"

"Love means that you care about someone a lot." She scratched at the side of her head. "And you want to be with them even if you can't be with them. You love them no matter what they do, whether it is good or bad."

"Whether good or bad?"

She nodded. "Sometimes I'm bad, and I get in trouble. But my eomma and appa always love me, no matter what."

"Because you are their life, living outside of their bodies?"

Bo-ah smiled at this and nodded quickly. "Yes. That."

CHAPTER SEVEN
A FIELD OF BEGONIAS

begonias are a warning of future misfortune

France

I gazed up at the large stone church. Arched windows of stained glass gleamed in the sunlight. Pigeons roosted on the ledges, backlit by beautiful reds, purples, and blues. The bells began chiming, sounding the midday hour and calling the faithful to prayer. All around me, the marketplace bustled with activity, buyers and sellers bickering back and forth as they attempted to either save or earn.

It was neither the toiling church bells nor the merchants and their stalls that I had come to the marketplace for but the pained soul I could sense like a fierce wave rolling through my chest.

I found the spirit without issue, wandering the streets of the marketplace. Pacing back and forth over the very spot where they had executed her. The ground no longer bore the scorch marks of flames, but the area was heavy with the presence of death. Many wandered here, tucked into crevices of the church or hidden down alleyways, their dark grey shadows so long gone I could barely catch their whispers.

Some were too saddened by their death, too traumatized to hear the words of release that I would speak. The spirit I sought today was not one of these. Instead, she bore her trauma aggressively, the shadow over her brightness a storm cloud of torment.

"Johanne." I called her name softly as I glided towards her.

She looked up, her eyes meeting mine in the distance between us, hatred and anger brimming in their depths. "They shall find no hand of redemption extended to them," she whispered to me.

There was a moment of recognition between us when I felt her understand who I was and what I offered. But that was washed away as she tipped her head back to begin screaming. Her hands fisted at her sides, arms painfully straight and her back arched as she wailed in agony, body writhing as if she were reliving the horror of her death.

In her despair, I sought to call out to her, trying to catch her attention and pull her out of the warped memory that trapped her. Instead, her screaming continued until she disappeared. Worried, I scanned the marketplace around me, searching for where her soul had reappeared. While it was not unheard of, it was not common for souls to relive their death, especially in such a torturous manner.

The strength of her continued torment concerned me. That level of darkness was never good, for this plane or that of the living.

While I could still sense her ailing soul, Johanne had not reappeared, and I sensed that she would not return to me today. She would be a slow and careful process as I attempted to bring her back from the brink of her fury.

Leaving the marketplace and the stone church behind, I made my way once more to that field outside of Orléans. In the months since that fateful battle, I had returned, speaking to those who wandered, lost to their unexpected deaths, trapped in a cycle that would not release them.

One had been receptive, listening as I called out to him, gradually allowing my words to sink into the heart of him.

"Hello, Charles." I stopped before the spirit, pleased to see that he was no longer stuck in his loop of searching.

Charles paused and glanced at me. "You've returned."

"I have."

"Is today the day?" he asked, gazing over the barren field.

Grass now grew bright and green over hills dotted with wildflowers where once bodies had lain bleeding and dying. It had been a much different sight back then.

"Are you ready to go?" I asked in return.

Charles lifted his hand up before him, twisting it back and forth as if reassuring himself that it was in fact still there.

"I believe so," he replied at last. "Is it terrible, where I am going?"

There was only a faint blue tint to his spirit beneath the dimmed grey shadow. "You won't be there long," I informed him. "You are almost ready for the Forever, and once you are ready to return, there will be no more suffering."

He nodded, and a sigh of relief slipped out of him. "I'm ready."

There was a peace in his gaze as our eyes locked, and it comforted me to see it. Moving closer to him, I rested my hand on his shoulder, murmuring softly. The peace remained as he went into the deep sleep.

My comfort over Charles was short lived as my mind returned to the marketplace and Johanne. Her torment was dangerous.

Korea

I drifted along the riverside, not interfering in Bo-ah's conversation with Sulli. I remembered how it had gone the last time and did not wish to tarnish what work was being done there. Perhaps Bo-ah would be able to help the young girl in ways that I was not able to, and when she was ready, I could help her transition.

For a little while, neither girl seemed aware of my presence, but then something—not movement because I had remained entirely still—captured Sulli's attention, and she looked in my direction.

Once Sulli was aware of my presence, it didn't take long for Bo-ah to turn her gaze upon me. She offered me a little wave and then turned back to her friend, who disappeared shortly afterwards.

I waited, giving Bo-ah time to make her way down off the bridge and to the riverside instead. Today, her clothes were more rumpled than usual, and there was a bruise and scrape on her cheek.

"What has happened to you?" I asked, a dark feeling swirling within me.

Her head tipped to the side. "Hm?"

I pointed to her cheek. "Your appearance. What has happened to you?"

Had those boys returned? Or perhaps another group of villainous children who did not understand her and wished to be cruel for reasons I did could not comprehend?

Bo-ah's fingers lifted to her cheek and realization dawned. "Ohhh. I fell out of a tree." A bright smile lit her face up as she uttered these words.

"A tree?" I frowned. "Who chased you up a tree?"

Bo-ah snickered at this. "No one. I climbed up because I wanted to! I wanted to see the city."

Her tone informed me that this was an entirely normal thing to do in her mind.

"Is this something children do often? You were in a tree the last time I saw you too."

"Yes."

It would seem children were even more confusing than I had previously thought.

"Why?"

"Because it's fun."

"But you fell and harmed yourself." The risk seemed to outweigh whatever fun could be had if you asked me.

"So? It happens sometimes."

"You could have died."

Bo-ah laughed and waved her hand at me. "You sound like my appa." Finding this highly amusing, she continued to laugh as she grabbed my hand and pulled me down to the water's edge.

I followed her, because it did not seem that I had much choice, and found comfort in this knowledge along with the solid strength of her fingers around my own. At the water, I stood there while Bo-ah picked up different stones and tossed them into the water. It seemed that she was looking for a particular sized splash, for as the splashes increased, so too did the size of the rocks she continued to find for herself.

There was something peaceful in the soft plop of stones into the lazy river, and rather than ask her what her purpose was, I simply enjoyed the moment instead.

Except that I was not meant for quiet times by the riverside, throwing stones and whispering into the winds. I was a collector of souls, and there was one in particular I could not forget. She found her way back into my thoughts, like a press of water finding a crack and slipping through.

"You're upset." Bo-ah was peering up at me, concern creasing her brow.

"I am not upset."

"You have worry lines in your forehead." Her small hand lifted to point at my brow.

"Do I?" My eyes lifted as if I would be able to see this crease of which she spoke.

Laughing, Bo-ah grabbed my hand and tugged me down to sit beside her on the riverbank. "What's the matter, Ephesus? Are you worried about something?"

I settled beside her, my dark robes tucked beneath my legs as I crossed them. "I would not call it worry, I would call it concern."

"Those are the same thing," Bo-ah argued.

I shook my head. "Concern is where it begins, worry is the outcome when it becomes something truly bothersome."

Bo-ah wrinkled her nose at me.

"What?" I asked her, reaching out to press a finger to her scrunched-up nose.

"Then what is *concerning* you?"

I shook my head. Gallus were not matters for human children to deal with. "Nothing you need be bothered with."

Bo-ah frowned, her eyes narrowing on me. "Tell me," she insisted.

"No." What could a child do to assist me in this matter?

It was my turn to frown, a gasp of shock slipping from me as Bo-ah struck me forcibly in the arm. I wouldn't exactly say that it hurt, as I was a being that could not be harmed, but it wasn't exactly pleasant either.

"Why did you strike me?"

"Eomma always says sometimes we need some sense knocked into us."

"Your eomma is a violent person."

This struck Bo-ah as amusing, and she giggled. "Now, tell me."

She was persistent, and beneath the sternness of her

childish gaze, I found myself unburdening the new concerns plaguing me.

"I've found a dimmed soul that I am concerned has suffered too much trauma."

"What happens when they have?"

I mulled over my response, wondering if I should be completely frank or if I should trim the edges of the truth. But looking down into her face, I saw the ways in which a spirit such as Johanne could be truly dangerous to Bo-ah and decided she should be made aware.

"They can become gallu," I explained.

Her brow furrowed in confusion, and I could see the questions spinning in her mind, so, before she could ask, I continued.

"When a spirit has suffered terribly in the plane of the living and dies in a way that is both tragic and horrific, their spirit is unable to let go. But it is worse than the other dimmed souls. This anger and betrayal can become so fierce that it lends a certain strength to the spirit, and they become gallu. Which—"

"Which is what?" she pressed, impatiently.

I frowned at her for interrupting. "A gallu is a spirit that has gained corporeal existence again and can interfere with the living plane once more."

Bo-ah's brows shot up, surprise on her face. "They can touch people?"

I nodded. "And worse, they can do harm, which is typically the desire of their spirits."

"Oh . . ." Bo-ah whispered.

"You must never interact with a gallu, Bo-ah. Understand?"

"But—"

"No." This time, it was I who did the interrupting. "There is nothing you will be able to do for one who has become gallu. You will know them by their anger, which is unquenchable. They are dangerous and will only harm you. Promise me that, should you ever come across a gallu, you will run away."

She did not look happy at this request, and I could tell she wished to argue the point. For such a young child, she had a strong sense of determination and dedication to those she was able to see in the plane of afterlife.

"Fine," she grumbled. "I promise."

"Thank you." I reached out to brush a hand over her hair, taking comfort in the contact.

France

"Johanne, please," I called softly. "Let me help you."

The spirit howled once more; her hands dug deeply into her hair, tugging on the strands.

"I led them," she wailed. "I led them! Victory! And then the pain! The fire! *The fire!*" Her screams filled the market-place yet again, and the flames ignited over her spirit, lighting the darkness around us.

CHAPTER EIGHT
DRINK A CUP OF CAMOMILE

*in the late 19th century, camomile meant
patience in adversity*

Korea

I had not returned to Wonju-mok in some time; years had little meaning to me as I wandered the earth, seeking out those who had need of me. But I found myself one day thinking of Bo-ah, and then I was there, in her small city.

She was now much grown, a young girl on the cusp of womanhood. It was surprising to see the youth gone from her cheeks as well as the innocence from her eyes. I had been gone much longer than I thought.

"Ephesus?" There was shock in her voice as she halted in her steps in the street. Then, seeming to realize she had spoken out loud, Bo-ah looked around us quickly.

"You have grown," I stated, moving closer to her.

She turned so that she faced one of the buildings to our right rather than the open street where anyone could see her, and I realized that she was hiding the fact she was speaking. It was my turn to look around us. The few people there were on the street paid Bo-ah no mind as they went about their day.

"You've been gone a very long time," she responded. Peering at me from the corner of her eye, she offered a soft smile, then nodded her head to the narrow alley. "Come, follow me."

Without waiting for me, Bo-ah headed down the alley-way. I found my fingers lamenting the loss of her childish hand slipping into mine to pull me along. Instead, I moved after her at my own pace.

When we came through on the other side, we were behind the shops, and there was a small path that led between those and a row of houses. Bo-ah waited for me to fall into step beside her before she continued on.

"It's nice to see you again." Her eyes did not have to drift upwards as far as they once had to find my face. "Why were you gone for so long?" she asked. "I kept looking for you . . . and I thought perhaps you weren't returning."

"I have a tendency of losing myself in the process of moving from one soul to the next. Time does not have the same meaning for me as it does for you," I explained. There was now a seriousness behind her smile that had not been there the last time I had seen her. "And I have never had a living soul to visit before."

Had I lost something intangible in missing out on the years of her growth? I felt as if I had skipped an important period of development that would help me understand the person she now was. Something in her countenance had changed from that youthful, spirited child I had grown to know. Her essence was still the same, but there was some-thing . . . a newness I had to get to know all over again.

"Well, then I suppose I cannot hold it against you." She offered me one of her bright smiles I remembered from her youthful days, which I found a relief to see, though it was tinged with that substance I was yet unable to place.

"I believe now is where I am meant to thank you?" I asked for clarification.

Bo-ah laughed, a true sound of amusement rather than expectation. "That is the proper thing to do, yes." She grinned and tucked a stray strand of hair behind her ear. "What soul did you come from this time?"

I frowned, thinking of the turbulent spirit I had visited before finding myself here in Wonju-mok. "A truly lost spirit that I cannot get to listen to me."

"Do they resist moving on like my friend Sulli?"

"She is different than Sulli. She does not cling to life, she clings to her death and the pain that it caused her. Each time I seek to speak to her, she bursts into flames."

"Real flames?" Bo-ah asked, concerned.

"Real only to her." Though her misery seemed only to grow. I feared one day her flames would break through to the living.

"I am sorry she is so lost to her pain. What will you do?"

"I will persist," I murmured more to myself than to her. There was little else I could do besides continue to show up in that marketplace. Letting Johanne know that she was not alone, and that I had not forsaken her as those in her lifetime had.

Suddenly, we were at an iron gate. Opening it, Bo-ah moved past the stone walls and into the garden beyond. Gliding through, I recognized the garden of her family home. She moved to a bench beside the small pond, and I let myself wander near the water.

"Have you been happy?" I asked at last. Bo-ah nodded her head in reply. "Have the other children become nicer? Or are they still senselessly cruel?"

"They are much the same, but I have gotten better at

hiding my conversations with the dead. Eomma was right when she told me they were better off not knowing what it is I can do."

I was happy to hear that she had found a way to exist without the torment from others.

"But you still talk to the spirits? To others besides Sulli?"

Bo-ah nodded. "I do . . . I have to pretend as if I don't though. I told Eomma that I had stopped." Her face saddened. "I don't like hiding the truth from her, but what else am I to do? They don't stop coming to me, and I can't simply ignore them."

"She fears for your safety?"

"She fears for my sanity. And what others will think of me. She says it was one thing when I was a young child and doing it, but now that I am growing up, it's not something others will look past."

I studied her, seated there on the stone bench. "This gift has not been easy on you." I thought of the boys with sticks.

"Is any gift that sets us apart truly ever easy on the one in possession of it?"

I did not have an answer for her, as I was not part of the human race, and so I looked down into the small pond instead. Another thought came to me then, one that I found I needed to ask.

"Am I a presence that makes it difficult on you?" I looked to her once more.

"What do you mean?" She frowned.

"You cannot tell anyone that you speak to me just as you cannot the spirits. You must hide our conversations. Would you be better off if I did not visit any longer?"

Just because she could see me, speak to me, and touch me did not mean that I had a right to be a presence in her life. Not if it would ostracize her from her own kind. Adding to the cruelty of her days did not sit well with me

"No, of course not!" She said it forcibly before biting down on her lip. Throwing aside her new air of maturity, Bo-ah left the bench and ran across the space between us.

I was surprised when she suddenly threw her arms around my form, her own slender body crushed against mine as she hugged me fiercely. I stood there, with my hands down at my sides, uncertain how to respond. This was the first time in my existence that someone had hugged me.

"You're my friend," she was whispering into my chest. "One of the longest ones I've had. Please don't leave me too."

Something of her words tugged at something inside me, and I found one hand lifting to rest gently at her upper back. "If you are certain I am not a cause for concern . . . then I will continue to return."

Bo-ah lifted her face from my robes and offered a relieved smile, some of that childish innocence from her youth returning, before the newfound maturity took its place. "Thank you."

I nodded at her, wondering what my presence could possibly offer one of the living.

"I've missed you, you know?" she stated. "Next time, don't stay away so long."

I felt chastened, and I also found that I liked it.

"I will do my best to pay more attention to the time."

Bo-ah simply nodded, then she rested her cheek to my chest once more and resumed hugging me as she was.

CHAPTER NINE
CLOUDS OF HYDRANGEAS IN VIEW

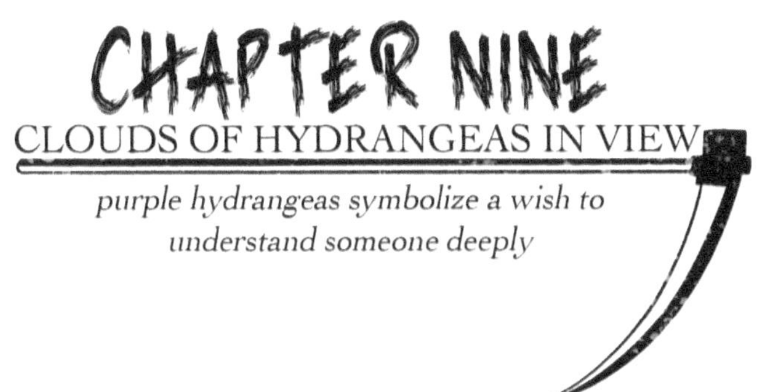

*purple hydrangeas symbolize a wish to
understand someone deeply*

France

I had not called out to her yet. Instead, I stood back, watching her progression round and round the market. Occasionally, she would stop to stare up at the church, her agitation only growing when she did.

It was the church who had found her guilty of heresy, sentenced her to death, and fastened her to the stake before the citizens of this very city. A people she had served and helped to lead to victory. Human behaviour was so willful and violent, undermining the greatness and selflessness of others with anger and misunderstanding.

Sometimes, I wished the Creator had not given them so much say over their own actions.

Today, the flames were not coiling over her form yet. But her agitation continued to grow, and unlike the other souls that I spoke to, she did not possess coherent thought. Her speech was warped by her anger and betrayal, and she rambled incessantly due to this.

I stepped up close enough that I could hear what she was

saying but was not directly in her line of sight. I wanted this to be a gradual process. If I could perhaps get her used to the feel of me there, then it was possible the sight of me would not be so disruptive to her.

"Heathen," she muttered, hands in her hair. "You're a heathen, Johanne. Women do not wear men's attire."

She paced before coming to stop directly over the spot where her execution had taken place.

"It was for protection. Protection." She whispered these words, as if trying to convince herself. *"Heathen!"* She shouted this up into the sky, her hands shaking in the air above her head before returning to her hair once more.

I moved closer, but this time, she took note and spun to face me. Her eyes were accusing, her lips pinched together.

"Johanne." I said her name softly, holding a hand out to her. "I am a friend."

She hissed and shook her head. "Stay away. Betrayer!"

She screamed and writhed once more as the flames overtook her. This time, there was a blackened spot of ash left behind on the earth when she disappeared.

Johanne was becoming more corporeal, and it would not be long before she had a firmer grasp on it. In her frantic state, there was no telling what damage she would do to the living plane around us.

I feared my own inability to stop her.

Moving on to my next soul, I felt the presence of something else, something *other* watching me. However, no matter how I searched, I could find no eyes to connect to that sense.

Korea

"I'm so glad you came today!" Bo-ah smiled at me. "I have someone I want you to meet. I think they are almost ready to transition on, and if you could explain to them what will happen, perhaps they would be willing."

I was not expecting to be led to a soul upon my arrival in Wonju-mok, but it was a happy realization that Bo-ah was now actively seeking to bring them to a place of acceptance.

"Take me to them," I stated.

Bo-ah grinned and motioned for me to follow her out of the garden into the streets beyond her home.

"How are you?" she asked me.

Blinking at what I still found to be an odd question, I found her peering up at me with interest.

"I have told you before, my state does not change."

Bo-ah shook her head. "I don't believe that."

This statement caused me to frown. "I cannot lie."

"I don't think you are lying, I just don't think you realize the ways in which you change or are affected. Last time you were here, you were concerned about your effect on my life. That shows that you worry and think of your own actions as they concern others."

I contemplated this. Did this mean that my own personal mental state could be altered more than I thought it could be?

"Have you been happy lately?" she pressed. "Have you been worried about the dim souls more than usual? Or have they been responding well lately?"

I thought of the never-ending search for those who had lost their way after death, and of Johanne in particular. The war that had cost her her life in the end was still raging on, had been raging on in different battles for over a hundred years and still did not seem ready to end.

"I do not understand the hatred of humans," I announced at last.

There was a sadness in her eyes as Bo-ah nodded in understanding. "Not many of us do. But what in particular has you troubled?"

Much like the last time we had walked, she led us down a path between homes where not many travelled, leaving us free to converse without fear of her being overseen.

"War . . . murder . . . jealousy and rage." I shook my head. "They are empty, terrible things that steal happiness and life with no true positive outcome. Why are the living so cruel to others around them? That is not why the Creator made you."

Perhaps this was a question not best asked of someone so young, but Bo-ah had seen and spoken to many in her short life.

"We're short sighted," she said softly. "We have a tendency of only being able to see what others have that we don't, or what has been taken from us rather than what remains. Life is short, and often we feel we don't have enough time to achieve what we wish to or what others expect us to."

The lifespan of a human was short when one considered the many years I had wandered this globe.

"Such a waste," I whispered.

"It is," she agreed. "So, you are not very happy then." It was a statement, not a question.

I thought of my own emotions, and the ones I had witnessed in the mortals around me. Though I wasn't always certain the things I felt were the feelings humans experienced, I knew the one I currently felt.

"I am happy to be here, with you."

This brought a smile to Bo-ah's lips. "I am happy you are here with me as well."

A silence fell between us as we continued our walk. We had come to a busier area of the city, and I did not wish to cause Bo-ah any hardships. Once we entered another back garden area, we were out of view of others at last.

The garden belonged to a large, sprawling home with several other small buildings on the property. A wealthy family lived here. It was not into the family home that we went, however, but to the small ancestor's shrine off the side of the main house.

On the steps sat an elderly spirit, her blue soul faintly dulled by a grey cloud. Bo-ah was correct in thinking that she was nearly ready to transition.

"Ah, agassi, so you have brought Jug-eum to me," she called out at the sight of us.

Bo-ah fetched up closer to her and bowed her head in greeting. "Yes, halmeoni. This is Ephesus, and he has come to speak with you."

She gazed back at me without fear, and with a wisdom that came with age. "What have you to say to me then, Ephesus?"

Grasping my hands together behind my back, I gazed down at her. "I have nothing to say, Eun Ae, but I believe you have a very important question to ask of me."

I could see it there, swirling within her. Her uncertainty and indecision over what awaited her.

Eun Ae motioned Bo-ah towards her, and once the girl was seated at her side, she took up her hand to hold it. Patting the top of her hand gently, the spirit eyed me. "This one came to me and gave word to my grief. Saw to it that my granddaughter knew my blessing on her wedding had been given in death, when I refused to give it to her in life." Eun Ae frowned, gazing out over the yard of her family home. "I refused to give blessings on many things that would make my family happy."

"You wished to see your desires carried out," I supplied.

"I did." She patted Bo-ah's hand almost absently, as if it were more to console herself rather than for the girl's bene-fit. "And I made life difficult for those I cared about, because

I believed my ways were the only way . . .and now—" She pressed her lips together, a deep frown over her face.

"You worry what that means for you in the afterlife," I finished for her.

Her dark eyes returned to me at last. She had ceased her patting of Bo-ah's hand and was now only clutching it in her lap. "Yes. Tell me, Jug-eum, what awaits me?"

I looked her over, noting the faint blue of her spirit beneath the dull cast of the dimmed. "You will not go directly on to the Forever." She nodded at this. "Instead, you will go into the deep sleep, and there you will dream of things, not so great things, that will help you to atone. Once you have done so, you will move on to the Forever and find peace."

She heaved a great sigh, though she did not need the oxygen. "How long will I sleep and dream?"

"I cannot say, for I do not know. That is not for anyone to decide but you and the Creator." It would all depend on how hard she fought against the lessons her spirit still needed to learn.

She turned to Bo-ah at her side. "What say you, agassi?"

Bo-ah smiled gently, and I noted how she squeezed her hand reassuringly. "What I have learned from Ephesus is that none of us can avoid what awaits us after death. Fighting against it and avoiding it only leads to more sorrow and pain. I think you are ready to handle whatever lays ahead."

Eun Ae chuckled darkly. "I appreciate your certainty in me." There was one more pat to Bo-ah's hand, and then Eun Ae stood. "Very well, Jug-eum, send me off."

I glanced at Bo-ah, wanting to make certain she, too, was ready to see her friend go. She only nodded.

Stepping up to Eun Ae, I rested my hand on her shoulder. "I will speak words, and then you will fade into the deep sleep. Go in peace, Sister, and rest well." I murmured over her and watched as the acceptance filtered into her eyes just before her spirit transitioned out of our plane.

When she was gone, I heard a sigh release from Bo-ah. "No matter how ready they are . . . I am always sad to see them go."

Without much thought in the action, I held my hand out to her. Bo-ah looked at it for a moment before standing to take it. There was a look of comfort on her face as she did so. Then, we made our way back out of the yard and to the streets once more.

"You are brave, to face the continual loss of friendships you make." It was something I was beginning to realize about her. To knowingly go into each new relationship with the intent being to help them transition away from this world, and to open her heart each time, meant she was always stepping into the possibility of pain in her fresh loss.

Most mortals avoided pain, some doing so with such a ferocity that they locked all others out simply so that they would not eventually lose them and feel that pain.

"Perhaps . . . but I have also been granted a gift. While it is a struggle, and it pains me, I also get to experience something precious." She looked up at me. "I'm simply grateful I have you to share this portion of myself with. That I'm not always doing it alone and hiding it."

"So am I," I announced to my own surprise.

But was it not why I had continued to return to Wonju-mok and to Bo-ah? Because here, in her friendship, I found someone who shared this experience with me, and it was something I had never before possessed in my very long existence.

CHAPTER TEN
LEANING ON THE ARBORVITAE

*arborvitae (tree of life in Latin) is a symbol
of strength, long life, and unchanging
friendship*

There was something about being in Bo-ah's presence that I could not resist returning to. Though I was visible to the dead, it was in Bo-ah's eyes I felt truly seen. Heard. Understood.

With the dead or dying, I was there only to help them transition, to understand what awaited them and aid them in reaching acceptance. But Bo-ah did not seem to need anything from me. Rather, she merely appreciated my visits for what they were. Time spent together.

A new question had begun to weigh on my mind. Were Bo-ah and I friends? I had heard so many spirits mention the great friendships of their life, and it was a relationship that was held very high in their esteem. Had I developed one without intending or even knowing how to?

Bo-ah, when I came upon her, was at the bridge once more, speaking to the spirit Sulli. As I approached, I noticed how Bo-ah now stood taller than Sulli, who had been older in spirit when they first met. Bo-ah had now grown past her in both height and age, Sulli forever trapped at the age of her young death. Pausing in my movements towards them, my head tilted a little as I gazed on them and pondered. How old was Bo-ah now?

At a person's death, I knew the intricacies of their life, the details of their very fibre. All of it I used to guide them into the afterlife quickly and efficiently. But the living, they remained a mystery to me, and I had always found it hard to gauge age, not that I had any need to know this detail of those who still lived.

Bo-ah now held a maturity to her that overshadowed the childlike demeanour of the spirit at her side. A wisdom that came from each new experience lived.

It was Sulli who took note of me, the easy look on her face falling away and one of distrust and uncertainty replacing it. Bo-ah noticed the change in her friend before becoming aware of the cause of it—me.

As she turned, a small smile appeared on her lips. Was this why mortals built friendships? Because the happiness of another person at the sight of you was a pleasant and heady thing? So many times I was met with fear or resistance when I came upon someone. Other times it was relief because I was there to help them slip away. But never simple joy.

This time, Bo-ah did not motion for me to wait. Instead, she waved her hand towards her, indicating that I should join the two of them on the bridge.

Sulli appeared hesitant as I glided over, but she did not disappear. This time she remained as I arrived at Bo-ah's side.

"I'm glad that you're here today, I wanted you and Sulli to have a chance to speak to each other," Bo-ah stated.

I looked between them, wondering what she thought the two of us would have to say to each other besides the obvious. "Why, is Sulli prepared to transition?"

"No," Sulli was quick to say, eyes turning on Bo-ah in an accusatory manner.

"No," Bo-ah said more softly. "But you're my best friends, and I thought you should know each other."

I blinked, a feeling of stunned surprise passing over me. I was one of her best friends? Me. The untried, inexperienced entity that was not human but was also not inhuman. How had I entered such a place of guarded respect? I felt a thrill of something pleasant passing through me. Warmth that buzzed and hummed through my being, filling me with a sense of wonder that made my spirit tingle.

From Bo-ah, my eyes travelled over Sulli, who did not look pleased to be sharing the title with someone such as me.

"I don't think that is necessary," Sulli responded and indirectly confirmed my suspicions.

Bo-ah frowned at this and sighed but did not press the matter. "We went to speak to Sulli's parents today," she announced instead, glancing my way.

"Together?" I questioned.

"Yes. Sulli wanted to be there in case they had personal questions I was not able to answer. At first, they didn't believe that I was speaking to them on her behalf. But eventually they came to realize she was there."

I frowned a little, listening to this as a new thought came to me. "I thought you were no longer telling others of your abilities for fear of what they may say or do." Didn't this go against her attempt at leading a normal life without the fear of bullies?

"I have to tell the families . . . or I can't help my spirited friends," Bo-ah replied.

Sulli simply continued to eye me with distaste. I withstood it gracefully. Souls had many different ways of receiving me, and not all of them were pleasant. Humans did not wish to die, even if it was onto a better, kinder place they were passing. The things of this life clung to them ferociously, and it could be a very hard time pulling free.

"Are you not afraid that they will tell your eomma? Or someone else?"

Bo-ah shrugged her shoulders. "They haven't yet. So far, they have all been very happy to hear the things that I have to tell them. Sulli's parents were so relieved to learn that it had been an accident that ended her life, and not her intention. They had lived so long believing they had failed her in some way." Bo-ah looked to Sulli, a kindness in her eyes. "I think it brought all three of them peace."

Sulli was also gazing up at Bo-ah with an endearing expression on her face. "It did."

Their friendship was real, that was easy enough to see, but it could also be a bane in allowing Sulli to move on to where she needed to be.

"So, you've done the thing that you both set out to do," I stated. "Does this not mean you are ready to transition on?" Despite what they had said moments ago, this made sense to me. "Is that why you've called me over here?"

Both girls looked at me with mixed expressions of horror and disbelief.

"No!" Sulli said at last, shrinking back and away from me.

Why did they always believe that I could force them to go? It had to be an acceptance within themselves or it would not work.

"We simply wanted you to know," Bo-ah chimed in with less force.

I did not understand. "But was that not what you were both waiting for? A time when you were able to find her parents and reveal the truth to them?"

"Yes—" Bo-ah began.

"It's not enough," Sulli interrupted her. "Over a loose brick, I never got to live. To grow, to experience. Through Bo-ah, I am able to learn what it would have been like if I had become a woman."

Bo-ah nodded her head. "I'm sharing my life . . ."

I could feel the contours of my face creasing with a frown as I listened to them. "That is not how this is supposed to work. We are only given the life we are given. We do not get to stay behind and simply watch through the eyes of another. That is not life."

I should know, for that had been my existence for centuries. Ever watching, but never living. Seeing was not living.

"Well, it's the only one I've got the chance to have." Sulli stepped back once more, her arms crossed stubbornly over her chest.

Bo-ah was looking at me, her eyes begging me to understand. But I could not support this, and so I shook my head.

"You will always be empty," I said to Sulli, gazing past Bo-ah and directly at her instead. "No amount of watching the lives of others can ever make up for the lack of experience in your own." I heard the hollow tone to my own voice and wondered when the emptiness had begun to settle in.

I didn't stay. I felt the unhappiness within both of them at my statement and felt it would be better if I left them to it. Sulli would need some time to decide for herself that the dregs of life she could take from Bo-ah would never be enough to make up for her death.

Egypt

Nassor stood watching his sons bathe his freshly fallen form: head, hands, and feet. He did not seem troubled, yet he did not appear ready to leave the process behind.

Silently, I slipped up beside him, coming to stand with my dark hands tucked into the sleeves of my robe as I, too, watched the cleaning process in preparation of wrapping his body in cloth. I could remember a different time when his family would have been spending this first day removing his internal organs from his body to set in smaller jars. However, just as mortals advanced and changed, so too did their burial customs.

"Has Allah sent you, malaikah, to bring me home?" Nassor did not look at me as he spoke.

"I have come on Allah's behalf, yes." The Creator had many names over the earth, all of them valid. "Will you go?"

Nassor shifted, grunting as his sons carefully and respectfully rolled his body to clean the back. "I spent all their lives trying to teach them respect, and it is only after I have died that they show me what I deserve." His voice was gruff with frustration.

His soul light was bright but tinged with a hint of blue. While he would not spend long in the deep sleep, there was yet a lesson he must learn there. I feared, though, if he spent too long watching his children with frustration that the blue would seep more deeply into him.

"The true sign of respect is when it is being shown to a person who is not there to see it. Your children respect you," I supplied in what I hoped was an encouraging thought.

Nassor snorted instead.

"You are a malaikah, what do you know of children?" He turned his head to look at me this time.

"I know only what I have seen in death," I said. Though I had learned somewhat over the years of watching Bo-ah grow. "But what a child does when their parent is not there to see is what they truly believe and feel." Of that I was certain.

Bo-ah respected her eomma's concerns for her life, but in the end went her own way when she felt it was needed. A parent's teachings could influence and sometimes dictate how a child lived, but in the end the decision was theirs to make.

Nassor grunted once more, then turned away from his sons. "Take me," he said.

I blinked, having expected more resistance from the gruff man.

"Very well." I stepped up to him, pulling my hands from my sleeves and reaching out to rest one on his shoulder. "You will feel yourself falling into a sleep. Do not fight it, or it will hurt. Simply go into it."

"A sleep?" Uncertainty filtered into his eyes at this.

"It is where you must go before moving on to face the Creator. It will make meeting the Creator all the sweeter," I assured Nassor.

With a nod, he relented. As he did so, I uttered the words that would send him into the deep sleep.

After Nassor faded away, I turned to watch his sons carefully wrap his entire body in cloth, preparing him for the grave.

There was no final resting place for my form, not in the sense that it was my own. Somewhere, my infant form rested with my mortal mother. Had I been mourned as greatly as she had?

Did mortals mourn those they had not even held?

CHAPTER ELEVEN

CORIANDER SHELVED

the coriander flower is a symbol of hidden worth

France

I stood before the church, gazing once more at the beautiful stained glass in the arched windows. The dark spirit of the troubled girl had called me yet again to the marketplace. Something of her turbulent nature was becoming a consistent worry on my mind. However, she was nowhere to be seen here in cobblestone streets.

I could feel Johanne, her torment tainting the air around the building before me, but she was not a physical presence in this moment. There was, however, another soul who was present, dark, curious eyes viewing me from the shadows of the cathedral.

The eyes belonged to a male, the faded din of his soul telling me that he had been lost to the shadows for a long time. Memories of his death returned to me like small leaves floating down from the sky: a young man who'd lost his life beneath the crush of a tipped carriage and a struggling horse.

Cautiously, I drifted towards him. Though he appeared interested in me, I did not want to startle him and cause him to flee. There were so many lost souls in this marketplace that I had not yet been able to reach, many of them castoffs from the cathedral, heretics who had died in horrible ways. This lad was simply one who had died too soon, and his soul had been unwilling to leave.

"Hello, Basile."

He watched me, staying hidden in the shadows cast off by the church.

"Have you come to stop her?" he asked.

"Her?"

"The one you seek is very angry. Her violence has only increased." His soul seemed to shiver as it flickered before me, apprehension there in the lines of his face. "Yesterday she caused a cart to shake, and one of the wheels broke."

My mind whirled, and had I a fleshy heart, it would have thumped more quickly in my chest. "Do you speak of Johanne?"

The young man merely nodded his head in response.

Johanne had made connection to the living realm once more. Her fury and anguish were so great, she was transcending what a dead spirit should be able to do. As I had feared, she was becoming a gallu.

"Thank you for telling me," I said. Looking at the soul, I took time to ponder his stance. "You needn't fear her any more should you choose to move on to the Forever."

He seemed to contemplate it for a moment, but then, with a silent shake of his head, he was gone. Something in this life was holding him here.

While I longed to help Basile, I had greater concerns to face. It had been a great deal of time since I had seen the formation of a gallu, and it did not rest well with me that one had developed now. I knew it would not please the Creator to see a soul so lost she had become violent.

Slipping out of the city proper, I went into the open fields where I could be away from the mortals and the wandering souls. I needed to connect with the great one. To see what I could do to prevent Johanne from ascending into true gallu status.

"Creator," I called out to the heavens above, closing my eyes as I did to concentrate better on my inner thoughts.

The Creator did not speak for ears to hear but for the mind and heart to feel.

"I need you."

Silence.

I waited, time passing all at once with an infinite slowness and an immeasurable speed.

"I do not understand what I need to do. I fear for what is to come. Please."

Still, there was only silence. Just a gentle reassurance humming through the worry and concern that I would see it done.

But would I?

Korea

The forsythia bush bloomed bright yellow, shining like gold in the afternoon sunlight. Gently, the blossoms swayed on their branches, while nearby, a black-and-white striped hoopoe oop-ooped beneath a plum tree. Its orange head—which threatened to compete with the forsythia—lowered back down to search for insects, forgetting the rest of the world for the moment.

It was a picture of life at its most vibrant, and yet I found the loveliest part of the sight before me was Bo-ah, laying on her back in the grass, her face pointed towards the sky.

I went to her, my form not casting a shadow as I came to

stand over her.

I was not sure what alerted Bo-ah to my presence, as there was no sound in my movements over the grass, but as I stopped beside her, her dark eyes opened to gaze up at me, squinting lightly in the sunlight.

She smiled as I came into focus, her cheeks creasing with happiness. There was a flutter inside me at the sight.

"Ephesus," she said joyfully.

"What are you doing?" I asked, looking her over before viewing the landscape around us once more. "Are you injured? Or simply tired?"

Bo-ah laughed softly at my words and, pulling herself up into a seated position, she smiled. "No, I'm just enjoying the sun."

"Enjoying the sun? How?"

Reaching up, Bo-ah grasped my hand and tugged on it gently, indicating that I should take a seat beside her on the ground. I questioned her judgement, but instead of voicing my concerns, I lowered myself to the grass.

"By simply absorbing its heat," she explained.

I glanced up at the bright round star in the sky and pondered what its heat might feel like.

"You're unable to feel it . . . aren't you?"

I simply nodded, holding my hand out before me, twisting it from palm down, to palm up. There was no change in temperature on my hand, no feel of the breeze around us or the prickly grass beneath me.

"What is it like?" I asked at last, looking over at her brightness rather than that of the sun.

Bo-ah tipped her head to the side in thought. "Well . . . like a gentle caress." She chewed her bottom lip for a moment and then reached out to gently brush her fingers down my cheek.

I was surprised by the light touch, as this was the first

time anyone had performed such an action towards me. Her fingertips were soft and silken, gliding over my cheek like a whisper in one's ear.

"So, pleasant then?"

Bo-ah smiled at this and nodded, her fingers gliding along my jaw once more before she dropped her hand into her lap, blushing a little.

"Why are you able to feel when I touch you but not the world around you?"

"I don't know. You shouldn't even be able to see me."

"Why were you created in such a way? To live but not to be able to experience?"A slight frown marred her brow as she questioned this.

I had never thought of it before, nor questioned the Creator's decision in making me as I was. But I had never had reason to question it before. Though the human world was a curiosity to me, I hadn't felt myself missing out until Bo-ah.

"It has never been in me to question why the Creator made me as I am . . ." Until now.

"Perhaps you should," she stated simply.

These thoughts made me uncomfortable. Was it my place to question the one who had given me the very life I led? I shifted in place, staring over at the swaying forsythia as I contemplated my inner turmoil.

"I apologize," Bo-ah stated softly. "I don't mean to upset you."

Shaking my head, I turned my gaze towards her instead. "Do you lay in the sun often?"

She followed the sudden progression of my subject change willingly. "No, Eomma fears the sun will blemish my skin with too many freckles. I am near the marrying age."

This announcement took me by surprise. I had not thought of Bo-ah to be at an age where betrothals could happen, though I knew she had grown. Would moments like this still happen once she was married? I had seen the changes that happened in a mortal woman's life once she belonged to her husband.

It was selfish to think it, but I did not want to see her married. Suddenly lost to me and taking with her this new version of the world I was just beginning to see through her eyes.

"Is that something you desire?"

"Freckles?" Bo-ah asked, a teasing smile on her lips.

"Marriage."

She sighed and reached down to pluck strands of grass from the ground, letting the gentle breeze carry them away from her fingers.

"It is the next step." Bo-ah halted, biting at her lip, dark eyes watching the last strand of grass blow away. "But I do wonder . . ."

I looked at her, encouraging her to continue. "About?"

"If I will find someone who understands me and what it is I can do." Her eyes filled with worry as she peered up at me. "I don't want to spend my life hiding who I am, Ephesus." Her hand lowered to press against her stomach. "The thought eats away at me and keeps me up at night."

"Will they let you choose?" I realized many did not get a choice.

Her frail shoulders shrugged. "They may ask my opinion . . . but it is their choice to make, for the best of the family."

I frowned, not approving of this idea that Bo-ah had no say in the future she would have. What of the ideas she had for her own life, or how she may wish to live it? Wanting to comfort her in some manner, I did something I had seen other humans do—I reached out and took her hand. It was a foreign action to me, and one I felt entirely inept to perform. While I had held her hand before, I had never attempted to offer comfort as I did now. I worried that I was doing it wrong, but Bo-ah seemed to appreciate it. Her fingers coiled back around mine in response, and she offered me a shy smile.

"I hope that you find someone who understands all that you are," I informed her. "My friend."

After all, that was who she was, was it not? My one human connection to this world.

"Thank you."

Having no other words to offer her, I remained silent.

We sat like that for some time, not speaking, just holding hands in companionable silence. In the end, it was Bo-ah who broke it.

"Did you mean what you said to Sulli on the bridge?"

"I always mean what I say." What was the point in lying? "But what, specifically, do you mean?" Many things had been said that day, and much of it had not been heeded by either of the girls.

"That no amount of watching human lives can ever make up for experiencing it yourself."

She fastened those dark eyes on me once more, and I felt them looking deeply into me, searching for an answer to a question I could not quite make out.

"Yes, I did."

Bo-ah suddenly appeared very sad. "I'm sorry Ephesus."

"For what?"

"That you have lived so many lifetimes and yet have never been able to truly experience what it means to be alive."

"So am I," I admitted—for the first time—to the both of us.

"Do you wish that you could be something other than what you are?"

It was a question I did not have an answer for, and yet I felt it was one that would remain with me until I did.

CHAPTER TWELVE
ANEMONES CRUSHED IN HAND

*the red anemone symbolizes both death and
forsaken love*

Greece

The cliffs before me were covered with small, white clay homes built into the sides of the rock, carrying all the way up the mountainous island. In the blue sky above, gulls cried their demanding screeches, searching the land and turquoise water below for any food that could be scavenged.

At the waterline of the white-sand beach, an elderly man stood knee-deep in the water, hands on his hips and his eyes squinting out at the calm surface of the sea. Koios Nephus had perished early in the morning while I was off convincing a young lass to make her way into the Forever. He was not one with a blue cast to himself; he had lived a good life.

"You don't look much like how I pictured Jesus."

His voice drifted across the water as I moved towards him on the beach, my feet leaving no footprints as I went.

"Because I am not he."

Koios looked fully at me, eyes dropping the full length of

me before drifting back up to my face. "You don't look much like an angel either."

"As I am also not."

Koios fell silent for a moment, simply studying me. "Have you come from the Underworld to collect me yourself, Lord Hades?"

I smiled as I shook my head. "I am called Ephesus, and I am not here to collect you but to help you let go."

"Let go." He shook his head, his hands shifting a little on his hips but remaining where they were planted. "I'm meant to see my daughter wed in a week's time, and I plan to be there to see it."

The important events were always the hardest for mortals to step away from.

"There will always be something else," I said. "If you remain behind for this, will that be enough?"

There would be babies to anticipate, birthdays to witness, great and important milestones not to be missed. Souls so easily became lost to these stages of their family's lives.

"Perhaps not," he responded. "But it is a day we've spoken about for such a long time, I can't miss it." He looked at me again then. "She'll know if I'm there or not."

Before I met Bo-ah, I may have argued this point, but now I knew some mortals were more connected to the world than I had thought. Perhaps his daughter would know if he were there watching from the soul realm.

"I will return," I told him.

Koios nodded. "Do. Perhaps when this is over, I will be willing to hear what it is you have to say."

Our eyes met across the softly crashing tide, and I nodded to him once more. "I hope that you are."

I turned from him then, to move on to another. There were plenty of souls on this small island to chase after. But something stalled me in my movements, causing me to look around.

There was a sensation of eyes watching me, creeping over my spirit. Tentatively I scanned the hillside, looking beneath the low-hanging trees and upon the cliffs above. There was no one but mortals going about their everyday business, none of them aware of my presence on the beach.

Yet someone, or something was definitely watching me with a cold, calculating glance that left me feeling uneasy.

Korea

I felt a tug on myself that was different from the calling of dim souls ready to find their peace. This felt more intimate and far gentler, though perhaps more insistent.

I knew exactly who it was calling to me.

And so I went.

Bo-ah had brought me to a small home on the outskirts of Wonju-mok that left me wondering how she had made her way out there on her own without anyone taking notice. She stood outside the small home, the bright colour of her red hanbok with its pale yellow jeogori standing out against the neutral backdrop of the house.

Beside her stood an elderly man whose soul was truly dim from years of resisting the pull of the Creator, but his eyes were calm and peaceful. Both appeared relieved when I approached and bowed slightly in greeting.

"You called?" I was surprised, as this was the first time I had truly felt her beckoning me to her side.

"Don't be upset with the child, Jug-eum, she only followed the request of this old Uncle."

I shook my head. "I am not upset, more curious."

"Dae-Hyun and I have been visiting for some time," Bo-ah began. "He is ready to proceed with you." She offered me a small smile with a tick of nervousness in the corner of her eyes that confused me.

There was no need for her to be nervous around me.

I nodded to the spirit. "Come, let us speak."

Dae-Hyun stepped away from Bo-ah, moving to my side, and together, the two of us began to walk a little. I could see the span of his life laid out before me, seeing the steps that had carried him throughout his time amongst the living and what had ended with his death.

"Tell me why you stayed."

There was a brief pause before Dae-Hyun responded. "I did not wish to leave my family. They depended greatly on me for guidance while I was alive, and I thought I would be able to remain a guiding force even in death."

"But you found you could not."

"I found everything we believe to be true is not."

I shook my head. So many different views on the afterlife existed all over the world. So many ideas on what happened once the soul left the body.

"Not everything," I corrected. "There are those with a strong enough will that return for another life."

Dae-Hyun glanced to me at this, and there was happiness in his eyes from this news. "I am pleased to hear it."

"But you are ready now? To leave your family and move on?"

He nodded his head. "I have watched my eldest son grow into the role I always hoped he would. I know they are in good hands now."

"In the end, the living will do whatever it is they will do, and there is nothing we of the non-living can do about it."

Dae-Hyun nodded. "That I have come to understand. The

little one helped me to see that I aided no one in staying here."

This made me smile, and I found myself looking over my shoulder to glance at Bo-ah, who stood with her hands clasped before her, waiting patiently for us to finish up.

"She likes to bring peace to the friends she makes in this realm."

"And she has." He was silent for a moment before continuing. "She told my son that I was proud of the man he had become and that he was filling my place better than I could have imagined. Somehow, she made him believe."

"She does manage to do that somehow." Even though her eomma wished for her not to speak of her spirit friends to anyone of the living. I stopped in our walking so that I could face him. "Are you ready now to transition?"

"Yes," came his easy reply.

"Do you wish to bid her farewell before you go?"

In a blink, he had disappeared and reappeared before Bo-ah. I turned away, giving them a private moment to say whatever there was to be said. When Dae-Hyun appeared before me once again, there was a quiet calmness about him that spoke of acceptance.

"I am ready, Jug-eum."

I lifted a hand to cup the side of his face and smiled gently upon his calm. "Be truly at peace, my friend. Your family will live their lives here as they see fit, and at the end of their days, they too will join you in the Forever."

Dae-Hyun smiled and closed his eyes. The smile remained as I spoke the age-old words, and he slowly slipped away into the brightness, drifting off into the space beyond.

When he was gone, I turned to face Bo-ah.

"I feel you should not be so far from home all on your own." I had never really scolded anyone before but found myself doing so now.

She only smiled a little before bowing slightly. "Perhaps not, but Dae-Hyun was in need of reassurance before he could be ready for you."

I moved closer to her until I stood over her, looking down at what were fast becoming endearing features.

"You will one day find yourself in a position of peril because you always follow the dim souls whether it is the smart thing to do or not."

Bo-ah had a moment of looking shamefaced before she sighed. "I simply have to believe that I have the ability to see them for a reason. And if it's not to aid you, then why?"

There were many questions I did not have answers to, and this was another of them.

"I do not argue your purpose," I said. "I just wish that you would show more concern for your own safety." I paused, taking a moment to study her. "I do not want to come here one day and find it is you I am helping to pass on."

I felt a chill pass through me, a dark message from something not so friendly, that one day it would be Bo-ah slipping away into the darkness of the sleep or the Forever. Gone from this world just like all the others.

I did not like to think on it. Even if it was the proper passage of time for all mortals.

This world would be a darker, colder place without her brightness to help fill it.

"I will be more careful, I promise." Bo-ah then surprised me by slipping her arm through mine. "Come, let's get back into town."

We walked in silence for some time, the weight of her touch on my arm something new and refreshing. Mortals often sought out touch, in both an intimate and friendly fashion. Hugs, hand holding, gentle kisses. Seeing it, I had never understood the appeal.

Feeling Bo-ah's slender hand on my forearm, suddenly I

was aware. There was a comfort in her touch that seemed to help steady the worried part of me that feared for her. Warm and solid, it connected me to her, and in so doing, reaffirmed that she was here and safe.

Was this what drew mortals into each other's arms? Was there safety and security in being held by those you cared for?

We didn't return to her home but made it to the field that I had found her in during my last visit. This time, we walked until we found ourselves amongst heavily blossomed trees. It was lovely and made Bo-ah smile.

As she lifted her head to peer up at the branches of the cherry tree, a petal fell and made its way to rest in her hair. Without thought, I reached out to brush it from her dark locks and found that the petal made contact with my fingertips.

Surprised, I froze for a moment, my fingers lightly touching her hair as they also touched the petal. Its softness was shocking, and the pad of my thumb brushed lightly over it until it dropped and floated down to the earth below.

My hand fell to my side as I stared in awe at the cherry blossom petal. How had I lived so long without ever knowing what a flower felt like?

"What is it?" Bo-ah asked softly.

"The petal . . ." I found I hadn't the words to describe what I'd felt or the new emotions washing through me.

She seemed to understand, for she smiled up at me. "They're softer than silk."

Bo-ah stooped down to pick one up off the grass and held it out to me. In response, I turned my palm up to receive it. However, as she dropped it, the petal fell through my palm, not even fetching up.

I stared at the space in my hand where the petal should

have been and sighed. Why had I for but a moment been able to touch it?

"Let's try something else," Bo-ah spoke. Stooping, she plucked up another petal. This time, instead of releasing it, she kept the petal pinched between her fingers as she ran it gently over the palm of my hand.

A startled noise slipped from my lips as I felt the end of the petal tickle my palm. Eyes wide, we both looked to the other, and in a moment of wonder, shared a smile.

CHAPTER THIRTEEN
PETUNIAS OF WRATH

petunias are a sign of anger and resentment

France

There was a dark cloud hanging over me that was not of the sky above but a sense of foreboding that led me back to the stone cathedral once more.

This time, Basile was not there waiting for me in the shadows of the church. I had not expected him to be. He was a weak soul in comparison to the fury that permeated this marketplace, leaving the stench of rejection and revenge clinging to the breeze.

Many of the souls who had once wandered this small space of the city had since disappeared, driven away by Johanne's presence. She was everywhere: in the lines of the street where helpless bystanders had stood, in the cracks of the cobblestone where soot and ash had crumbled, in the wooden shutters stained from years of smoke.

I waited, a steady presence in the middle of the marketplace, gazing up at the bell tower that sounded out the morning hour. All around me, mortals went about their day-to-day business of living, completely unaware.

I felt angry eyes along the back of my neck before I saw her. A dark, ominous cloud of despair and wrath levitating over the heads of the humans.

Her body was not fully formed, her spirit too fractured to actualize her calves and feet. Though she had hands, they were burnt and blackened, skin peeled away from her bones at the tip. This shouldn't have been so; injury did not follow death.

"Why must you come to torment me?" Johanne screamed through a mouthful of flames, her hair rippling in the heat of them.

"I do not seek to torment. I wish only to bring you peace, Johanne."

She shrieked, hands suddenly bound behind her back as her body writhed in agony, head angled up towards the sky. "Why hast thou forsaken me?!"

I watched in abject dismay as Johanne's spirit was engulfed in flames, her form thrashing against unseen bindings that held her in place. She was reliving her death yet again, trapped in this infinite loop of painful memory.

Just as the fire reached its climax, Johanne rushed me, catching me unawares. Without time to react, I braced for impact, feeling her fiery form pass through me. I staggered, taking several steps to the side in order to regain my stance and feeling within me the clinging effects of Johanne's anger. I felt tainted by her touch, the spread of her fury a threat to my own peace of mind.

"Johanne!" I called out to her, spinning around to watch her progression across the marketplace.

To my further horror, she collided with mortals, forcing them to physically stumble back and a child to drop onto their bottom. Cries of surprise and fear rang out as the people searched for the presence that had knocked them to the ground.

"Maman!" a little girl cried out, reaching for her mother, who quickly scooped her up into her arms.

People began to flee, which only intensified when Johanne passed through a fruit stand, causing the woven baskets and the tabletop to burst into flames.

More screams rang out as men and women fled the scene, fire licking along the table, reaching for another. Shouts for water were heard, and two men hurried to grab a nearby horse's trough and bring it over to the fruit stand. Others grabbed sheets and blankets, beating at the flames to try and keep them from spreading.

There was nothing I could do about the fire. But I could attempt to halt the culprit in her tracks.

I followed Johanne down an alley between the church and another stone building. She was dragging burning fingertips along the outer wall, which thankfully could not ignite.

"I know you're in pain, Johanne. But the Creator wishes to ease that. To send you into a deep sleep. The Creator wants you to make your way back to the Forever, to be with the rest of them." I kept my voice calm, inviting, even if the scene behind me had left a sour taste in my mouth.

Gallus were dangerous, and Johanne had grown into a full version before my eyes.

The very thing I was meant to prevent. Had my attention been elsewhere too often? Learning about a world I could not be a part of, yet which enticed me. Following smiles and gentle touches. Filling the void of curiosity until I was full.

The gallu turned on me, hissing. Her eyes glowed in the dark pallor of her face. "You wish to further torment the heathen. I saved you all, and yet you want nothing but to punish me! Endlessly!"

She howled, her head tipping back as she raged at the heavens. Perhaps her cries would reach the Creator and they would be answered.

"Johanne," I tried once more.

This time, instead of responding to me, she disappeared, melting into the side of the building but leaving in a way that left a heated hollow space where she had been.

Sighing, I hung my head. This should never have been able to happen. My role here was to make certain that distraught spirits did not get to the point where they were able to make contact with the living world.

Yet, here was Johanne. Screaming, knocking people over, and lighting the world on fire.

"I've failed you." I said the words quietly, but they were meant for only one set of ears. With everything, I waited and listened. Hoping to feel that gentle caress of another presence around me. To feel the relief of comfort inside me as the Creator responded.

Silence.

"I don't know how to help her."

I'd never known one to be quite so destructive. Fire was an entirely new aspect to gallu that I hadn't seen before. Violence against the living world was not new, but setting things aflame was. It made her dangerous in a whole new fashion.

When I was certain there would be no response, I began to make my way through the city streets, seeking out those who I might actually be of use to.

As I went, I felt an angry presence following me, the heat of eyes on the back of my neck watching while I spoke with other spirits and visited with the sick and dying. In this moment, she wasn't corporeal, so there was nothing I could do to hunt her down, but Johanne was a taint on each visit that was made.

I had thought to go and see Bo-ah once my time in this city was done, but I could not be certain where Johanne was or how far she would follow me. Would her wrath lead her out of the city and into the wide world?

Could I carry her with me through to other nations? To other people whose homes and lives would be disturbed? Would she be a blemish on each death and passing that I was present for?

I could not risk leading her to Bo-ah. Not today. Not after everything else.

CHAPTER FOURTEEN
TEETERING ASTERS ON A SHELF

*given their name after the Greek word for
'star' due to their shape, asters stand for
love, wisdom, and faith*

Korea

The gallu had followed, appearing in the least expected places. Not a constant presence, but enough to keep me away from Wonju-mok.

The dark energy coming off of her was troublesome. Each place she appeared, a small fire would erupt, the living would be attacked, and eventually, someone would wind up screaming and running for their lives.

Worst of all, I had no idea how to stop it.

Johanne was fierce, distraught, and unreasonable. Her pain had taken her to a place that I couldn't seem to bring her back from. And still, the Creator remained silent. I tried my best to believe this meant I held within myself the means of fixing all I had let go wrong, yet I wasn't so sure.

No matter my attempts at contact, Johanne remained impenetrable.

I had just eased a dim soul into the deep sleep when a

firm tug came at my centre. Unlike the gentle calling of before, this was fierce. Emotional. Needy.

Fearing the worst, that Johanne had found Bo-ah despite my distance, I hurried to Wonju-mok, heeding the summons of Bo-ah.

She was beneath our cherry tree, looking troubled but uninjured. Still, I moved quickly to her side, my hands grasping hers tightly.

"Is everything okay?" I asked, tension filling my spirit.

Bo-ah offered me a small smile that did not reach her eyes and furthered my concern. She had been happy the last time we stood beneath this tree. Happy and relatively carefree as we marvelled over my ability to feel the petal.

"Things have changed," she said haltingly.

"What . . . things?"

"My eomma and appa have found me a prospective husband." Her voice was soft, careful, hesitant. Dark eyes flicked back and forth between mine as she waited.

"No." It came out forcibly, in a way that shook me to the core, for I had not even meant to say the word.

Bo-ah startled a little, her fingers tightening on mine as her eyes widened slightly.

I shook myself, trying to ground the foreign frenzy growing inside me. "You said that it was a thought for the future, not that it was something to happen today."

"It is still a thought for the future," she said carefully. "But they have found a high-ranking man of the jungin, one who holds a place of authority. He is looking for a wife."

She appeared calm, but I had grown to know her enough to recognize the unexpressed emotions coursing beneath the surface. I had felt it in the call when she'd summoned me.

"You don't want this." She couldn't. I knew of her fears. Knew what marriage to a man of stature in the mortal world could do to her. She would not be able to speak to the spirits that sought her out. Would not be able to admit to seeing things no one else could.

She would not be able to meet with me in gardens and watch the softness of a flower petal transform my world. I felt a sinking feeling in the pit of my spirit. A sense of loss that was new to me and which I did not want to continue. Bo-ah had become my special friend, the one human I had been able to remain in contact with.

I did not want to lose that.

"I don't know what I want—"

"You *can't* want this. What about—" In my haste, I had interrupted her, but only now did I realize where my own thoughts were taking me. A place I had no right to contemplate, let alone enter.

"What about what?" she pressed.

"Your gift," I said instead of the other thoughts swimming around in my mind.

Bo-ah shook her head. "I don't know." There was a deep worry in her eyes. "I don't think he is someone who would understand what I can do. If we are to marry, I don't know that I can continue to do any of this."

"Tell them no," I was quick to insist. If she refused, this wouldn't have to be an issue. And I could stop this growing ache inside me from spreading.

Bo-ah scoffed a little, pulling her hands free from mine as she shook her head. "It's not that simple, Ephesus. It is my family's duty to find me a husband, and it is mine to accept the one they choose."

"But they are choosing the wrong one!" I felt anger surge inside me. Yet another new form of human life I had not properly experienced before. How could she simply accept what she did not want, what would make her unhappy?

"Are they?" Her eyes bore into mine, seeking, questioning. "What if this is what is meant for me? You yourself have questioned why I continue to do what I do, even when it causes trouble with the living world."

I had said such things to her, but she was younger then. More impressionable and yet wholly determined to continue.

"You have never ceased, no matter how many times I've told you the way of things. You always set out to change them and do as you see right. Why is now different? Why would you abide by what they wish when it is not what you want?"

"Because life is not easy for a young woman on her own!" Her cheeks were turning red, the flush spreading down her throat. "And I cannot always have what I want." Bo-ah's hands slipped into mine once more, and I accepted them greedily. "Can you offer me another solution?" she prompted with a whisper.

I stared, confusion swirling.

What solutions could I give when I knew nothing of the inner workings of a family mind, or even the true processes of the society in which she lived? Their deaths I understood. It was their lives that still puzzled me.

"Ephesus?" she prompted me, soft but pressing.

Her eyes, which peered back at me, made me feel exposed, open to her examination in a way that I had only felt before with the Creator. There was a power in her words and the clutch of her hand.

"You are mine," I rasped. Blinking as her eyes widened a little, I rushed on. "My connection to this world. Through you I have learned more of life than I ever did in all my years alone. I believe . . ."

"What?" Bo-ah whispered.

"The Creator sent you and your gifts to show me what it was like to be human."

It felt like revealing a great vulnerability to say it out loud and yet a relief as well. Releasing one of her hands, I raised my palm to cup her cheek. Skin as soft as a cherry blossom, I couldn't help but think that Bo-ah was more lovely than all the flowers this earth had to offer. Through her eyes, I had been given witness to just a fraction of what it meant to be alive. Yet it had been more than I'd ever had before, and it was enough to make me crave more.

"If you marry him, I will lose you."

Bo-ah's eyes filled with tears as she leaned into the press of my hand. Her own hand lifted to slip tenderly around my wrist. "I know." Her words came out rough and pained. "I don't want to."

A great wave of relief washed over me as she admitted this at last.

"Then don't. Tell them no."

Her eyes shut as she continued to lean into my touch. "But what will I do? Will you take care of me?" Her eyes opened to peer up at me.

What could I do? I had no connection to the mortal world beyond what her presence afforded me. But surely there was a reason Bo-ah had come into existence. That lovely, twinkling spirit that had pulled me towards her from the very beginning.

"There will be a way. I am sure of it. The Creator has a purpose in all things," I assured her.

Bo-ah smiled softly and nodded a little. "Okay. I will not abandon you, Ephesus."

I surprised myself then by leaning in and pressing a kiss to her forehead. Her cheeks flamed with a bright flush at the action, and her head bowed in shyness.

"I must go," I informed her. "I can feel the call of souls who are in need of me."

Bo-ah nodded. "Go. I should be on my way home now, before Eomma grows suspicious."

As I pulled away from her, I felt a shadow of something behind me. A chill coursed up my back, and turning, I sought the bushes and trees around us. There was nothing there that I could take note of, but the apprehension had now settled over me.

"Be cautious going home," I told her. "Remember what I said, do not approach spirits that seem unsettled. They are not all kind as your friends have been."

"I know, I will be careful."

Nodding, I turned from her then. I still felt the darkness in the corners of my mind, enough so that I did not wish to leave Bo-ah on her own. But there were many souls the world over who had need of me, and I could not ignore the need of the dying for one of the living. No matter who she may be.

Italy

Alfonse had slipped away into the deep sleep after some pressing. His own acknowledgment of how terribly he had lived his life had left him fearing what awaited him beyond.

Fear was a very tangible reason for remaining and kept so many souls from transitioning. In the end, it had only taken the assurance that it would not last forever but that the deep sleep was only a stage of purification before he was ready to rejoin the other souls in the Forever.

As he disappeared, fading into his sleep, I gazed up at the starry sky above me. If ever there was a time when I had need of reassurance myself, now was it.

"Tell me, what is to be done for Bo-ah?" I watched the twinkling stars and the bright spots of blue glowing souls as they fell to the earth to find their awaiting hosts.

I thought this was going to be another moment of silence when nothing came, and I would be left to sort it out. But then I felt it: the swell of peace within me and the reassurance that when the time came, I would know what was to be done.

Smiling, I moved on to my next soul.

CHAPTER FIFTEEN
HANGING DRIED ROSES

*the fragility of a dried white rose stands for
death being preferable to losing your virtue*

Korea

I shouldn't have left. Not without first warning Bo-ah of the dangers that had been stalking me. But there had been no reason to believe that the gallu would make it there on her own.

I felt the spike of fear the moment Bo-ah called to me, my name a tragic plea for help. It was infectious, spreading through me as I rushed to Wonju-mok.

Though I had known what to expect when I arrived, it was still a shocking sight to find Bo-ah cornered in her garden, pressed against the brick wall, with the gallu floating angrily over her. Why Johanne had sought her out, I would never understand beyond a sense of hatred for me and my inability to aid her.

"Johanne," I called out her name.

Both the gallu and Bo-ah glanced in my direction, relief brimming in Bo-ah's eyes, while Johanne's burned with rage.

"Why must you follow me here?" she shouted, half-turning away from Bo-ah to glare at me.

Johanne's hair filled with flame, the locks licking along the air, searching for something to feed on. From her head, the fire travelled down her shoulders and along her torso, heading down her legs.

I could feel what I could only assume was heat wafting off the fire even from many feet away. It caused concern for Bo-ah, who was much closer and very much still alive.

"I came because I was needed," I began carefully. "I don't wish to harm you, Johanne I only want to help you."

"Help me?!" she shrieked into the air, her voice loud enough that it broke into the living realm and startled some birds out of the tree above. "They all claimed to help me, only to use me." Her eyes hardened on me. "You've come to take your fill of the heathen, haven't you? Used for my leadership, to win, until there was no more need of me. Now here I am, rotting in this dungeon . . . *attacked* for trying to maintain my purity. The slacks do not take from my love of God! I won't allow you or any of the other guards to take my honour from me!"

I shook my head, raising a hand slowly in the air. "No . . . I don't wish to take anything from you, Johanne. And I know that you're not a heathen. You did what you believed you were called to do."

Over the gallu's shoulder, I made eye contact with Bo-ah and then looked to the empty space to her side where she could hopefully dart away from Johanne. Nodding slightly, Bo-ah began to slowly shuffle along the wall.

"*It was the truth!*" Johanne wailed. "Not just what I *believed!* God spoke to me!" She moved closer to me, clearly wishing to make me feel her pain and frustration.

The heat of the fire enveloping her pricked along my cheeks, but it relieved me. The closer to me she moved, the farther from Bo-ah she got, and the more likely Bo-ah was to be able to flee.

I kept my eyes on Johanne's, not allowing myself to look in Bo-ah's direction, even though I wanted to be certain that she was fleeing. "I believe you," I said cautiously.

Johanne paused, her body rigid but her eyes intent on my face. "You do?"

"I do."

"Will you tell the others? The king? The pope?"

Lying wasn't a part of my vernacular. There was no point in lying to those who were already dead, not when they must be willing to move on to face what was to come. But in this instance, would lying be beneficial, or cause more harm?

My hesitation was all it took. Bo-ah's toe hit a small stone, and the sound of it scattering away caused Johanne to whirl around on her.

"No!" Her shrill cry sounded out as she dove for Bo-ah.

To my horror, I watched her seize Bo-ah's wrist in her burning hand, wringing a cry of agony from her lips. Bo-ah being harmed was the last thing that I had intended, and I simply could not stand there and watch her life end in such a tragic way. Life without her in it would become unbearable. Though it was one day inevitable, I did not think this was how the Creator had meant for her life to come to an end.

Not knowing what I was doing, I rushed Johanne and, wrapping my arms around her from behind, I pulled her away from Bo-ah. The tackle surprised the gallu, who released Bo-ah's arm. Pulling her injured wrist to her chest, Bo-ah sunk to her knees in the garden.

Johanne and I fell to the ground, barely stopping at the soil, but thanks to Johanne's furious solidity, we rolled. She fought with the ferocity of a caged wildcat, body thrashing against me while her footless legs kicked at my own calves.

I had not expected the pain on my own part. But there was something so tangible about her pain and fury that made it real even for me. As her flames licked and bit along my chest and arms, nipping at my cheeks and tearing at my hair, I continued to hold her.

"Johanne, Johanne! Please calm, it will be okay!"

"No!" she cried, continuing to fight.

"It will be!" The heat stung my throat, coiling inside of me. "I vow it. Let me help you. Let me help take the agony away." My arms tightened around her, simply holding her as she fought.

Her screams eventually became tears, and her struggles gave way to sobs. With her fight ended, I loosened my arms just enough to be only there for comfort. "The Creator loves you," I murmured near her ear. "You aren't meant to stay here in this pain. You are meant to go home, home to peace and happiness."

She cried all the more, the flames dying away from her body. "I only did what I was supposed to," Johanne sobbed.

"I know," I soothed.

"And they took me to the stake . . . I fought so very hard to save them all, and then they betrayed me."

"I know." All I could do was agree and reassure her that I understood her plight.

Gradually her sobs relented and a sort of calmness overcame her. When I was certain she was no longer a danger to Bo-ah, I released her, and the both of us sat up to face each other.

"It can truly be over?" she asked, hope shining in her tear-drenched eyes.

I nodded. "It can." I reached out my hand to cup her cheek. "Let me send you home. Back to the Forever."

"Reaper," she whispered, understanding finally coming into her eyes.

I could only smile gently.

"I'm sorry."

"I know."

"I never meant to cause anyone any harm."

"I know that too." My hand dropped to her shoulder. "May I?"

This time, it was Johanne who nodded. "Please. I am so very tired."

I began to chant the words, watching as she closed her eyes, and finally, a long sought-after peace filled her features. As she began to dissolve, I felt my own relief washing over me. She would not go to the Forever straight away—there was still plenty of healing that would need to happen for her in the deep sleep. But eventually she would be released from all of her burdens and find herself where she had always belonged.

CHAPTER SIXTEEN
A FIELD OF FORGET-ME-NOTS

My spirit ached in a physical way it never had before. Singed deeply from Johanne's flames, I stiffly rose to my feet, wincing at the truly unpleasant sensations. So, this was pain. I could see why mortals wished to avoid it at all costs.

"Ephesus!"

Hearing my name on Bo-ah's lips, I spun to face her. Without warning, she launched herself into my arms, curling up against the still smoking folds of my black robes. I held her tightly despite the pain of it and buried my face in her hair.

She smelled of something sweet and earthy, and I wanted to hold on to that scent forever, as well as the feeling of her tucked safely in my arms. How could something feel so right and yet be entirely wrong?

I shut my eyes against the new pain coursing through my soul, hurting more deeply than the flames had ever dared to. So, this was heartbreak. The inner turmoil that drove people to desperation and sometimes death.

"I knew you would come," Bo-ah rasped into my chest, her voice muffled by black cloth.

I smoothed a hand over her hair, feeling the way she leaned against me so trustingly. My words in the garden came back to haunt me, a whole new torment of promises that must be broken and the recognition of demands that never should have been made.

"I am so sorry that I led her to you." My hand drifted down to her wounded wrist, and gingerly, I lifted it up so that I could see the angry welts and blisters forming along her pale flesh. Would this mar her? Leave her burdened with further disdain from others?

Just how much pain could I bring to her life?

"That wasn't your fault," Bo-ah insisted.

"Yes, it was." I stepped back enough that she could see my face clearly. "I failed to help her because I was distracted, and then I led her straight to you. I knew she was following me . . . and still I came at your call."

"Ephesus . . ." Concern began to fill Bo-ah's eyes as realization started to dawn in them.

"I mustn't risk it again."

Her breath hitched, and Bo-ah shook her head. "What are you saying?"

"I can't return to you after this."

She gasped and shook her head. "Don't say that. You are . . . you are my . . ."

"It is because of who you are to me that I cannot return."

Bo-ah tucked her injured wrist in against her chest once more, holding it there as tears welled and she fought a swell of her own emotion. "But in the garden, you said—"

"I know what I said." I swallowed against a rise of something in me that wished to burst out. A surge of emotion so strong, I thought it capable of sweeping me away in the tide of it, taking me down into a darkness that was eternal.

"You said I was your connection . . . You can't just go away." Her bottom lip trembled, and it sent a fresh pang coursing through me. "You are the only one who understands what it is I do. You are the only one who understands why I must do what I do. *You said you didn't want to lose me!*"

All of it was truth, and none of it could be denied. But all of it was the very reason why I knew I must step back.

This wasn't the outcome I had envisioned as I prayed into the sky, seeking the help of the Creator. But I knew it was the truth of our situation now. I was not meant to be any longer a part of this current life.

"And I do not." I moved towards her, but she stepped back, avoiding my reach. I halted, abiding by her obvious need for space. "But that is why I must leave. There will be others. Other spirits I cannot calm, whose ire I raise to the point of attack simply because of who I am and what I must do for them."

Bo-ah simply shook her head in denial. "How many years has it been? This is the first that it has ever happened!"

"Perhaps," I replied sadly.

"I can't lose you," she whispered, a tear slipping down her cheek.

I moved then, unable to stop myself, and reached out to cup her cheeks, holding her precious face between my palms. "Your life can be normal. You can live the life you were meant to live. I was selfish in thinking that I could offer you the fullness of a life you deserve. Bo-ah, I cannot. I am not even alive. I am not a healthy friend for you to have."

Her lip trembled once more as her sadness escaped, breaking the part inside of me that should have been a heart if I had been a living man.

"But . . . the garden. I don't understand."

I pressed my forehead to hers. "I want to see you always," I admitted at last. "But I cannot be the reason that your life ends too early. I am not meant to be a part of your life any longer, Bo-ah. I was wrong to press you for more than what you are capable of giving."

I could feel her body shaking from the tears, and it tore me apart.

"I will always be in the way of your friendships with the living, and that is not fair of me to ask of you."

"But it is something I am willingly giving!" Her hands grasped onto the front of my robes, pulling on them.

I smiled through the pain and kissed her brow. "I know."

It changed nothing, and we both knew it.

"Then what was it for? What was *any* of this for?"

Life. Love. Experience.

"You were my gift," I said simply. "For a brief moment in time I was allowed to have you as a part of my existence. I had a connection to this human world, to the smells and touches. To the emotions that fill all of you to the brim. Do not underestimate what you brought to me." My voice broke, and I pressed my forehead to hers once more, feeling the soft exhale of her tears against my lips. Was this love? "You brought a world of change to my existence. Please don't let mine be the end of yours."

She only shook her head, then buried her face in my chest, tucking herself into my robes once more. I held her for some time, until her tears had run dry, and I felt the hollowness of it within myself.

Gradually, Bo-ah pulled away, her cheeks tear-stained and pale. "Thank you for being a part of my life while I had you." Her voice was soft and raspy.

"Promise me something?" She nodded. "Stay away from the angry spirits. I know I've said it before, but I cannot say it enough. Remember today . . . Don't let them pull you into something you cannot escape from. I want you to live a full and long life."

"I promise. Only my sweet friends who need assistance."

Needing to feel the solid presence of her one last time, I brushed the back of my knuckles over her cheek.

"Goodbye, Bo-ah."

"Goodbye, Ephesus."

I left then, before I could second guess my actions or take back my words. The years she had already given were more than I could ask for, and now she was free to be what she was meant to be.

I felt the rightness of it deep within me, the acknowledgement from the Creator that this was what had been intended. But it did not ease the pain.

For once, I truly knew what it was to be alive.

EPILOGUE
AN ORCHID BLOOMS

*traditionally, pink and white orchids are a
sign of sympathy, as well as being a symbol
of eternal love*

Outside the door sat three bowls, one of vegetables, one of rice, and one of soup. Beside each sat an envelope of money and a pair of shoes. I brushed my foot over it all, watching as it passed through them without touching. How pointless it was to have set these items out for Death when I could not even receive them.

Yet, had she still been here, I could have.

"I thought I would find you here," a voice spoke from behind me.

Turning, I found Sulli, still as young and innocent looking as the day she had died but with a seriousness to her eyes that denoted the years of her existence. I faced the house once more, listening to the sounds of the women preparing the burial feast, led by the eldest son's wife.

"She is already gone," I said. "If you were hoping to keep her here with you."

"No." She had come to hover beside me on the step. "Bo-ah was ready to leave."

She had lived a long life. Marriage. Children. The life a living human woman was meant to carry out. I had watched all of it from the shadows, jealous of the happiness her husband brought to her and the love I watched blossom there. I had watched, never imposing but always aware. And like a lovely potted orchid blooming beneath the scrutiny of the gardener, eventually the blooms must wilt and the petals fall.

"And you?" I glanced to her, feeling an unruly sense of jealousy fill me.

Sulli had stayed beside Bo-ah all through her years. Experiencing each new stage of life as her living friend did.

"I, too, am ready."

I thought I had seen the resignation within her being.

"Was it worth it?" I asked.

There was silence for a moment until, at long last, Sulli responded. "No. It was never enough."

I could only agree. What little taste could be given to those of us who did not live could never be enough to make up for the lack of actually living. And now Bo-ah too was lost to both of us. The one connection to the living that either of us had.

I felt a hole taking form inside of me, one that unsurprisingly bore the shape of Bo-ah. The world seemed to have lost its sparkle now that she was no longer in it, and I couldn't help but wonder, who could ever hope to fill the space she had left?

"Come," I said to Sulli. "It is time we sent you home."

1. Welcome to the Black Parade by My Chemical Romance
2. What Sarah Said by Death Cab for Cutie
3. Land of Confusion by Hidden Citizens
4. She Used to be Mine by Jessie Mueller
5. Who Wants to Live Forever by Queen
6. Til it Happens to You by Lady Gaga
7. There's a Man Going Round Taking Names by Johnny Cash

ACKNOWLEDGMENTS

As always, I want to thank you, the reader, for picking Ephesus' story out of all the other potential stories to read. I hope that you enjoyed following along on his path of self-exploration. His story is not over, and I hope you will join both he and I on our journey through the rest of this series.

Thank you to my beta readers, Elle, Lou, Candace, and Tanya. You were the first eyes to see Ephy, and you helped me to fine tune him. You also helped talk me through the writing of this when I tried my best to get in my own way with self-doubt. Thank you for being an amazingly supportive team!

Special thanks to Yeonwoo, who took the time to read this and offer her special outlook as a Korean citizen. It meant a lot to have your blessing on this manuscript.

Once again I owe a HUGE thank you to Lou Wilham for helping to bring my vision of the Ephesus cover to life. What would a girl do without you?

And Meg, you helped give a final polish on this bad boy. For that you have my gratitude.

ABOUT THE AUTHOR

 Christis Christie was born and raised in a small town in New Brunswick, Canada where she spent most of her time either reading someone else's book, or dreaming of writing her own. Her favourite thing to dive into is an epic fantasy, or anything else magical and wondrous that really allows her imagination to take her away.

She now lives on the East Coast in Halifax, Nova Scotia where she works as an event designer, putting her interior decorating degree to wonderful use. Whenever she's not busy magically transforming venues for her clients, Christis is working on her own writing.

Her other dreams consist of one day visiting Ireland so she can frolic over the hills, and owning a teacup Pomeranian she can cart around everywhere with her.

THE PRINCE OF STARLIGHT
THE HEIR TO MOONDUST: BOOK ONE

LOU WILHAM

Prince of Starlight by Lou Wilham

An outbreak of strange curses. A kingdom in chaos.

With the kingdom of Lunette's people in peril, their prince has one choice. Aided by his best friend and protector, knight Dame Ignacia, Prince Cricket—young, cheerful, and oft-times ridiculous—set out in search of answers.

Swords and opinions clash as Cricket and Ignacia work together to solve the mysteries that surround them. But they must set aside their differences to find the culprit before the perpetrator can launch their next attack on Lunette and plunge the kingdom into darkness.

A frolicking LGBTQ+ fantasy novel steeped in action, wit, and all of the corniness. Perfect for fans of Terry Pratchett's Discworld, Neil Gaiman's Stardust, and William Goldman's The Princess Bride.

Add to your TBR
Available Dec. 15 2021

The Bone Valley by Candace Robinson

He's a lover. She's a thief. A magic like no other will bind them together.

After the death of his parents, Anton Bereza works hard to provide for his younger siblings. Love has never been in the cards for him, especially after desperation forces Anton to sell himself for coin. And he has no idea that, beneath the city of Kedaf, lies a place called the Bone Valley.

When Anton's jealous client plots against him, he is cursed to spend eternity in a world where all that remains are broken bones. There, Anton meets Nahli Yan—a spirited woman who once tried to steal from him—and his cards begin to change. But as the spark between them ignites, so does their desire to escape. All that stands in their way is the deceitful Queen of the Dead, who is determined to wield her vicious magic to break Anton and Nahli apart. Forever.

Available Now

The Castle of Thorns by Elle Beaumont

To end the murders, she must live with the beast of the forest.

After surviving years with a debilitating illness that leaves her weak, Princess Gisela must prove that she is more than her ailment. She discovers her father, King Werner, has been growing desperate for the herbs that have been her survival. So much so, that he's willing to cross paths with a deadly legend of Todesfall Forest to retrieve her remedy.

Knorren is the demon of the forest, one who slaughters anyone who trespasses into his land. When King Werner steps into his territory, desperately pleading for the herbs that control his beloved daughter's illness, Knorren toys with the idea. However, not without a cost. King Werner must deliver his beloved Gisela to Knorren or suffer dire consequences.

With unrest spreading through the kingdom, and its people growing tired of a king who won't put an end to the demon of Todesfall Forest, Gisela must make a choice. To become Knorren's prisoner forever, or risk the lives of her beloved people.

For fans of Sarah J. Maas, Jennifer Armentrout, A.G. Howard, Casey L. Bond, and Naomi Novik.

Add to your TBR
Available Nov. 3 2021